GEO

What About
CIMMARON?

D0956263

What About CIMMARON?

LAURAINE SNELLING

JOURNEYFORTH

Greenville, South Carolina

Library of Congress Cataloging-in-Publication Data
Snelling, Lauraine.
  [Tragedy on the Toutle]
  What about Cimmaron? / Lauraine Snelling.
      p. cm.
  Originally published: Tragedy on the Toutle. Grand Rapids :
Baker Books, 1982.
  Summary: After the 1980 eruption of Mount St. Helens, thirteen-year-old Sarah Sorenson finds her faith tested as her family is
forced to evacuate their Toutle River Valley home, leaving behind
their cattle and her beloved horse, Cimmaron.
  ISBN 978-1-59166-872-5 (perfect bound pbk. : alk. paper)
  1. Saint Helens, Mount (Wash.)—Eruption, 1980—Juvenile fiction. [1. Saint Helens, Mount (Wash.)—Eruption, 1980—Fiction.
2. Volcanoes—Fiction. 3. Trust in God—Fiction. 4. Christian
life—Fiction. 5. Family life—Oregon—Fiction. 6. Fathers and
daughters—Fiction. 7. Horses—Fiction. 8. Toutle River Valley
(Wash.)—History—20th century—Fiction.] I. Title.
  PZ7.S677Whc 2008
  [Fic]—dc22
                                              2008013297

Cover photos: iStockphoto.com © Michael Fernahl (boards),
  © Manuel Ribeiro (horse); USGS/Casades Volcano Observatory
  (eruption)

Originally published in 1982 as *Tragedy on the Toutle*

Design by Nathan Hutcheon
Page layout by Michael Boone

© 2008 by BJU Press
Greenville, SC 29614
JourneyForth is a division of BJU Press

ISBN 978-1-59166-872-5

15 14 13 12 11 10 9 8 7 6 5 4 3 2 1

To the Maries in my life—mothers, daughters, friends—
Especially my daughter, Marie,
who gave me such joy during her too short life.
And to Marie, who shared her daughter Cecile with me.

CONTENTS

Author's Note

Mount St. Helens, a pristine peak in western Washington State north and east of Longview, began experiencing internal quakes deep below the surface in 1979. The quakes led to explosions of ash, sending columns that looked like concrete miles into the atmosphere. No one knew when or if the mountain would really erupt until the Sunday morning of May 18th when the entire north face blew out, leveling timber for miles and sending huge boulders, ash, and melting snow into the rivers. The Toutle River raged into the Chehalis and thence into the Columbia River, the water hot enough to boil fish, and silt filled the shipping channels. The Toutle Valley filled with mud and forever changed the lives of those who lived there. The ash from the eruption spread east, inundating Eastern Washington and trailing in the stratosphere clear to Europe.

We lived north of Vancouver, Washington, and watched much of the early explosions, some from our back yard as the columns and clouds rose miles into the heavens. On the Sunday of the eruption, we were one of the last cars let through before the I-5 freeway was closed due to flooding and bridge damage. We'd gone north to Silverdale, Washington for a family event. Spirit Lake and Mount St. Helens were favorite camping places of ours so we'd driven the road up there many times. The destruction was beyond words. And so my story of Sarah and her horse, Cimmaron, was born as we watched the news with rescuers pulling cattle from the mud.

Lauraine

CHAPTER 1

"Can you go riding right away?" thirteen-year-old Sarah Sorenson asked her best friend.

"Hope so. I'll call ya." Jani's smile lit her sparkly brown eyes.

The bus stopped. Sarah grabbed her books as she stood up. "What about you guys?" She glanced at the two boys slumped in the seat across the aisle.

"It all depends."

"Yeah, I know. Call me." Sarah pushed past the knees in the aisle to follow her sister, Kathy. "We could go way up that new logging road if we hurried." She shot a grin over her shoulder.

"Don't go too near the mountain, Sarah. I heard warnings earlier." The bus driver smiled. "And you be good, Kathy."

"Thanks." Sarah jumped the last step. The April afternoon sun struck gold in her feathered hair.

"Call me right away," Sarah called to the faces at the open windows. The red lights stopped flashing as the yellow bus pulled away. Sarah waved again and ambled across the black-top road to get the mail.

Fence rail-thin, nine-year-old Kathy waved one last time, then streaked down the rocky driveway. "Race you to the house!"

"You cheated!" Sarah shifted her books to the other arm and trotted after her.

Sarah breathed deeply. Spring, sure enough! No wonder the cows were getting fat. The grass smelled so good that Sarah was tempted to eat it herself. She stopped and pulled up a juicy grass stem. Trying to figure a way to get both chores and riding in before dark, she nibbled on it, hardly noticing the yellow daffodils fencing the white, ranch-style house. Further down the hill, the faded red barn might as well have shouted at her, *chores first*!

"But I *am* going riding," Sarah promised herself as she pushed through the split-cedar gate and ran down the sidewalk. Yellow and red primroses lined the cracked concrete.

"Kathy?" Sarah bounded up the three cement steps and burst through the front door.

"Back here." Kathy's muffled voice came from the direction of the bedroom.

Sarah paused to read the note on the maple kitchen table.

"Dishes, bathroom, bedrooms . . . it's just not fair," she muttered. "I've *got* to go riding. But there's always housework."

Sarah hated coming home to an empty house. Before Mom went to work at the savings and loan in Longview, there were always cookies baking and the good smell of dinner. Lots of times, Mom sang her "Jesus songs." Best of all were the hugs and the "how was your day," no matter what she was doing.

Now there was just the empty smell and feel of a no-one-home house. Sometimes Sarah didn't even want to come home. Especially if she couldn't ride.

She crumpled the offending piece of paper and chucked it at the wastebasket. It bounced off the rim. Sarah glared at the wadded paper and stamped down the hall.

"Kathy, would you do all my housework today? I just have to go riding."

Kathy shook her head.

"But I haven't gone riding for ages," Sarah pleaded.

"No way."

"I'll do your work tomorrow."

"That's what you always say."

"But I really will."

"Sure you will."

"All right! Be a brat! See if I do anything for you again." Sarah slammed the door as she hurried to the kitchen to answer the phone.

"Toutle Farm." She raked her hair back.

"Sarah, I can go." Jani's excitement bubbled over the wire.

"So can the guys."

Sarah groaned.

"What's wrong?" Jani's enthusiasm slowed. "Can't you go?"

Sarah bit her lip. "Mom left a list a mile long. It'll be at least an hour."

"But that's too late. I have to be home by five."

"We won't have any time."

"What about Kathy?"

"Oh, not today. She won't help me at all."

"Sarah, couldn't you ride now and do your chores really fast when you get home?"

"Well . . ." Sarah's thoughts scampered around like gerbils in a cage. She knew the rules. Chores first, then play. But how would *they* ever know? She'd get back and work like crazy.

"I can't," she said flatly. "Kathy'd tell."

"Bring her along. She can ride our pony."

"Just a minute." The receiver bounced on the counter. Sarah ran down the hall. "Kathy? Want to go riding with us? You can borrow Andersons' pony."

Kathy jumped from the bed, her forgotten book flopping to the floor. "Now?"

"Yep, hurry and change. We don't have much time." Sarah raced back to the kitchen to grab the phone. "It's OK. We'll be right over. Call the rest of the gang."

Sarah flew down the slope to the barn. Her high-low whistle for Cimmaron cut the afternoon stillness.

A soft nicker replied from the corral behind the barn. Sarah whistled again as she reached inside the barn for the bridle hanging on a nail beside the door. On second thought, she stepped inside to the covered barrel for a handful of rolled oats.

"Hey, Cimbo," she whispered as she rounded the corner of the barn.

The bright sorrel gelding stood at the near fence of the corral, head over the bars. His ears pricked so far forward that they nearly met; his white blaze, from ears to nose, sparkled in the sun. Both wide nostrils quivered again in a soundless nicker.

Sarah stopped in front of him, her hands behind her back. "Which one do you want?"

The horse paused a moment before pushing her right shoulder with his nose.

Sarah held out her right hand. Empty! Cimmaron shook his head, forelock swinging over his eyes. Then he pushed again, harder.

"You silly," Sarah said, laughing. "Don't like to lose, do you?" She held out her hand. Cimmaron munched the oats, his whiskery lips searching out every grain.

"Come on. We gotta hurry." Sarah unhooked his halter and hung it on the fence post. She slipped the bit in his mouth and the headstall over his ears. As soon as the gate swung open, Cimmaron danced through.

"Really want to go, don't ya?" She chuckled.

Sarah tied the reins through the ring beside the barn door. Cimmaron stamped impatiently while she disappeared inside for the saddle.

"Not bareback today," she said as she lugged the saddle and padded blanket out and dumped them, horn first, on the ground. "Besides, Kathy and I'll be riding double as far as Jani's." Cimmaron's ears moved back and forth in time with her voice. Sarah heaved the saddle over his back. Cimmaron grunted as the off stirrup thudded against his ribs.

"I'm sorry," Sarah murmured, patting his shoulder. "Just trying to hurry." She pulled the cinch tight, separated the reins around his neck, and swung herself up. Both feet in the stirrups, she nudged her willing horse into a canter up the slope to the house.

"Come on, Kathy," Sarah called.

Kathy charged out the door, her ponytail bouncing as Sarah pulled her sister up behind her.

"You ready?"

"Sure." Kathy wrapped her hands in the latigos behind the saddle seat. "May Rex come?"

"Nope. Rex, stay home," Sarah ordered the gray-mottled cow dog. Ears down, Rex lay in the dust and watched the girls ride off.

Dusk was falling as Cimmaron trotted back down the driveway, his shiny coat dark with sweat.

The red pickup was parked in its usual place.

"Boy, we're in for it now," Sarah whispered. "Wouldn't you know? Dad's home early tonight."

Kathy sniffed and scrubbed away a tear. One scraped knee peeked through the ragged tear in her jeans. The matching scrape on her chin still oozed.

"I'm sorry," she whispered back. "I didn't mean to fall off."

"Of course not," Sarah comforted her. *But it sure did slow us down,* she thought. *Dumb pony! If he'd just stood still. Taking off down the trail like that; I could have beat him bloody.*

The girls dismounted in the barn's shadow. While Sarah unsaddled her horse, Kathy opened the gate.

"What's the meaning of this?" Ted Sorenson's voice was sharp with disgust. His corked boots moved soundlessly down the slope. Worn jeans and faded plaid shirt under wide suspenders completed the picture of a logger.

"Oh, hi, Dad." Sarah hefted the saddle and blanket and eased toward the barn.

"Just a minute, I'm talking to you!" Her father's command rang out.

Sarah flinched. *Here we go again*, she thought as she threw the saddle over its barrel.

"I thought you had chores to do."

"But . . ."

"But nothing! You were supposed to do them first."

"But you got home early."

"That has nothing to do with it." Dad's voice grew louder. "I've told you . . ."

Sarah glared up at her father. His blue eyes, so like her own, flashed icy sparks back at her. A gasp cut off her words as she saw the mountain behind him.

"Dad, the mountain!"

"Sarah, you're interrupting!" he thundered.

"But, Dad, look!" The shock on Sarah's face forced him to turn around.

Sunset-pink Mount St. Helens, once snow-capped and serene, looked like a giant had stuck a monstrous concrete pillar in her crest. As the three stared, the pillar grew, the plumes at the top reaching for the heavens.

Kathy inched closer to her father, pushing her hand into his. Absently, Dad hugged her close.

Sarah couldn't believe it. Sure, the mountain had been steaming for the last few weeks. The scientists kept saying she would erupt, but no one paid much attention to them anymore. Everyone had gotten used to the steaming and the minor earthquakes, or temblors as the experts called them.

"My mountain," Sarah gasped.

The three of them turned as the green Pinto wagon braked to a gravel-spattering stop by the pickup.

"You've seen it then," Mom called as she climbed from the car.

"Mom, were you watching it from the beginning?" Kathy ran to meet her. Hands locked together, the two russet-headed members of the family joined Sarah and Dad at the barn.

The mountain and its still-growing pillar were lighted by the setting sun. The Sorenson family stood close together; fear and awe circled around them.

"What did you hear on the radio?" Dad finally asked.

"Traffic is stopped all over Portland, any place people can see the eruption. The interstate bridge is one huge jam."

"Sure glad you didn't have to come through that." Dad squeezed Mom's slim shoulders.

"But what about our mountain?" Sarah turned from staring at the peak.

"No one knows for sure what's gonna happen." Mom shrugged. "Right now, reporters keep announcing how high the ash is going and the wind direction."

"I'm scared." Kathy snuggled between her mom and dad.

"But no one's mentioning damage," Mom finished.

The four watched as the mountain faded in the dusk. The top of the cloud of billowing ash and steam still glowed in the sunset.

Cimmaron blew on Sarah's neck, then shoved at her arm.

"Yeah, come on. I'll put you out in the field. You've been pretty patient." Sarah led her horse through the open gate before she took off the bridle. He rubbed his forehead on her arm one more time and trotted off to join the cows.

"You think they'll be all right, Dad?" Sarah motioned toward the grazing animals.

"I hope so." Dad and Mom started toward the house, arm in arm. "Oh, and Sarah." He turned back again, his mouth stern. "No riding for a week."

"But . . ."

"No buts. I mean it. You broke the rules again."

CHAPTER 2

Saturday morning, May 17, at Toutle Farm, bacon, eggs, and pancakes with lots of syrup welcomed the family.

"Breakfast's ready." Mom wiped her hands and sat down.

Sarah rubbed her eyes, yawned and stretched, then slid into her chair.

"I'm going riding right away." She reached for the pancakes.

Her father laid his fork down with a clatter, a frown creasing his forehead. "Not today."

"But, Dad!"

"Not today, Sarah. Your mother needs help around here." His voice got louder. "All you ever want to do is ride."

"I'd work faster later," Sarah bargained. "It'll probably rain again this afternoon."

"The sun *is* shining, dear." Mom smiled across the table.

"I said no! That's final." Dad pushed back his chair. "At least not until all your chores are finished. It's time you learned to be responsible." He stamped out. "I'll be working on the tractor," he called as the back door slammed.

"Why is he so mean?" Sarah moaned. "He never wants me to ride Cimmaron. And it's so nice right now." She ran to the large picture window. "Look, you can even see the mountain."

"Be patient, Sarah," replied Mom. "He's worried about the river flooding."

Sarah reveled in the scene before her. The hill that snuggled around the house fell away to flat pastures dotted with white-faced Hereford cows, all with romping calves. The Toutle River, swollen with glacier runoff, marked the far side of the property. Beyond the river, the tree-covered hills led to graded larger foothills. Dingy-gray Mount St. Helens crowned them all. It had been nearly a month since the original blast. The news kept saying there could be more.

Sarah checked on her mountain every day. Sometimes she caught only a glimpse. Other times the peak hid behind clouds and rain. Then there were days like this one. Even ash dirty, Mount St. Helens stood out against the azure sky.

"Well," Sarah sighed. "Let's get going." She glanced down to the horse, peacefully grazing. "He'll probably forget those lead changes I taught him." She turned to her mother. "I haven't ridden for a whole week."

"Then let's get the chores done quickly so you can go," Mom replied. "Call Kathy. She needs to help this morning too."

Sarah headed for the bedroom the girls shared.

"Come on, lazybones." Sarah yanked on the covers. "You can't sleep all day. You can even see the mountain."

"What time is it?" Kathy yawned.

"Past breakfast, and we've got chores to do. Hurry! I want to go work Cim." Sarah opened and slammed drawers. "Dad was really a bear this morning."

"Has Sunshine had her calf yet?"

"Nope, at least Dad didn't say so. Now hop to it." Sarah finished pulling on her jeans and hurried back to the kitchen.

Mom put down her coffee cup. "Sarah, why don't you start by vacuuming the living room? Kathy can do the dishes as soon as she eats. Make sure all your laundry is in the hamper first."

"I already did that. What else has to be done?" Sarah squared her shoulders as the list grew. She'd have to hurry if she wanted to ride at all. Things just weren't the same since Mom went back to work.

Several hours later, Sarah stepped out the back door and looked to the west. What a break! No clouds. Her piercing whistle floated across the pasture, answered by a whinny. She ran down to the barn. Bright red ears perked, waiting for a second whistle. When it came, Cimmaron trotted to her, his sorrel mane ruffled in the breeze. Sarah's eyes glistened at his effortless gait, his two white socks dancing through the grass. What a horse! Just enough Arab mixed in with the Quarter horse to give him style.

"You look classy." She laughed as Cimmaron nuzzled her shoulder. "But you're just a big baby." Sarah scratched his ears. Cimmaron blew gently in her face.

"Come on." She grabbed his halter and opened the gate.

Sarah brushed and saddled Cimmaron, and in minutes they were cantering across the pasture. The cows raised their heads. The calves, tails in the air, raced away in mock terror.

Sarah counted the cows. Only fifteen, one missing. *Where's Sunshine?* she wondered.

Sarah and Cimmaron angled back to the hill. Thick fir trees covered part of the pasture, a favorite place for the cows when calving.

"Come on, Cim. Let's work on those leads again. Hope you're as smart as I think you are."

Cimmaron cantered slowly up the rise. Sarah leaned to the left. Cimmaron began to lead with his left front foot. After a few paces, Sarah leaned to the right, gently laying the reins to the right at the same time. Again the horse changed rhythm, this time leading with the right foot. Neither time did he stumble. By the time they reached the trees, Sarah barely moved left or right to keep Cimmaron dancing along. She pulled him to a stop and hugged him.

"You were great." Cimmaron's ears twitched at Sarah's compliment. "Now let's find that silly cow."

Moving up the hill, Sarah checked each patch of brush. Tall evergreens blocked the sun to make shadows. Halfway up the hill, where the rocks began, several fir trees had fallen.

In the small clearing, sparkling with sunlight, a white-faced cow licked her still-wet calf.

"Oh, Sunshine," breathed Sarah. "He's a beauty."

The cow rumbled low in her throat. Pushing hard with his back legs, the calf struggled to stand. He took one step but all four legs bent beneath him and down he crashed. Sunshine licked him again, all the while encouraging her baby with soft moans. The calf knelt on wobbly front legs. He pushed again, to stand swaying in the sunlight. Step by step, he stumbled to Sunshine's udder, and bopping and pushing, began to nurse. His white-tipped tail flicked from side to side.

"Let's go get Dad," whispered Sarah. She and Cimmaron trotted back down the slope.

"Dad!" Sarah called as Cimmaron cantered up to the fence.

Dad pulled his head from under the tractor engine. "Now what?" He straightened with a grimace. "Why are you riding? Are those stalls mucked out yet?"

"But, Dad . . ." Sarah wailed.

"You know that's one of your Saturday jobs."

"I thought I could go when I finished helping Mom."

"You don't think. You just do what you want without asking. When are you going to think about other people?"

"But, Dad, Sunshine had her calf . . . up in the trees."

"Go get Kathy. She can help bring them down. Then you get at those stalls."

"But . . ."

"Sarah!"

Sarah slipped off Cimmaron. "What a grouch," she muttered as she threw the reins over the fence. She kicked the stirrup that dangled in her way as she lugged the saddle back to the barn. Fathers sure were hard to get along with—at least lately hers was.

That evening, after the table was cleared, Dad opened his Bible for family devotions. "Tonight we'll read from Psalms again, where God talks about protection."

Sarah drew circles on the tablecloth with her fingernail. Dad's voice grew distant as she remembered Cimmaron and his quick uptake on the lessons. Maybe tomorrow she could . . .

"Sarah," her father's voice broke into her daydreams. "Were you listening?"

"Uh, sorta," she mumbled.

"I hope so," Dad sighed. "Let's pray." The family joined hands around the table. "Father, I confess that I have been impatient with my family . . ."

Has he ever, thought Sarah. *But why confess it? Nothing changes.*

"Sarah, do you have anything you'd like to pray about?"

"Uh, thank You, God, for Cimmaron and our ride today. Uh . . . amen." Mom squeezed Sarah's hand.

"Kathy?"

"Thank You for my baby chicks and for Sunshine's calf, amen."

"Thank You for taking care of us, Jesus, and giving us promises of Your protection," Mom added.

With the final amen barely out of her mouth, Sarah jumped up and headed into the living room. Soon the rest of the family joined her.

"Sarah, did you get the shavings hauled into those stalls?" Dad asked.

"I will tomorrow, right after church. I ran out of time."

"Dad," Kathy asked, "Sunshine's calf is really a beauty, isn't he?"

"He should be, with those bloodlines. Maybe you'll be able to show him at the fair, then sell him as a yearling bull."

Sarah glanced at Kathy. Thank you, she mouthed. *That had nearly set Dad off again*, she thought. *He never picks on Kathy like he does me.* Sarah ran slender fingers through her wind-tousled hair. Just because Kathy was the baby and she was older. No matter how much she did, it never seemed to be enough. And the work never seemed to end.

Sarah crossed the room and turned on the television.

"Switch on the news." Dad looked up from his paper. "See if there is anything new about the mountain."

"Down at the grocery store they have the evacuation routes posted." Mom picked up her crocheting.

"The rumblings have settled way down again." Sarah sat down cross-legged in the middle of the rug. "There haven't been any eruptions for over a week."

"I'll be glad when this is all over," Kathy shuddered. "All you hear about is the mountain."

"Dad, a bunch of us planned an all-day ride on the logging roads next weekend if the roadblocks are lifted." Sarah bit her lip. "May I go?"

"All you loggers are back to work," Mom put in.

"We'll see," Dad mumbled. "Next Saturday is a long way off."

CHAPTER 3

Be-e-e ba-a-a, Be-e-e ba-a-a, the high-low screams of the police-band scanner shattered the Sunday morning peace.

"The mountain!" Sarah cried. Her hairbrush clattered unnoticed to the floor as she raced down the hall. She nearly collided with her mother as they hurried to the picture window.

"What's going on?" Kathy shouted from the shower.

"The mountain blew," Sarah yelled back. "Hurry up."

Sarah and Mom stared at the roiling gray-black pillar of ash and steam that resembled an atomic mushroom cloud. Higher and higher the monster writhed above Mount St. Helens.

The scanner continued to squawk. The clouds grew and spread, filling the horizon.

"Mom, look," Sarah whispered. "Dog's Head. It's disappearing." Slowly, as if the scene were being filmed in slow motion, portions of the mountain slopes disintegrated.

"Get your dad. He's down at the barn."

Sarah flew out the door. She ran down the slope as though an avalanche were right on her heels.

"Dad," she panted as she wrenched open the barn door. "The mountain blew."

"What'ja say?" Dad called from the hayloft. "It's not time for church yet."

Sarah darted to the ladder and clambered up. "The mountain . . . Dad . . . the mountain blew. The evacuation signal is coming over the scanner."

"Dear God." Dad instinctively turned in the direction of the swiftly-changing peak.

"I didn't hear anything," he mumbled as he and Sarah climbed down the ladder. A shower of hay seeds raced them down. "I really didn't think it would blow."

Swiftly Dad closed the barn door. Father and daughter sprinted up the hill toward the house. Dad turned, halfway up the grade.

"Dear God," he whispered again. The monumental black mushroom dwarfed the trees, fields, and valleys between the Sorenson farm and Mount St. Helens. The early morning May sun hid behind the turbulent mass.

"God, help us," Dad breathed as he turned and ran for the open kitchen door. In the blossom-covered apple tree, a single robin chirped, then—silence. Rex, his blue eyes pleading for attention, slunk onto the porch, right on Dad's heels.

"Oh, Ted." Mom ran to his arms.

"Daddy, I'm so scared." Kathy's brown eyes filled with tears.

"It's OK. God is right here with us." Dad, with an arm around each of them, crossed to the window. Sarah turned again to the awesome eruption. How could he be so calm? Her teeth chattered. She hugged both arms to her chest. Huh . . . God hadn't had to take care of an erupting mountain before.

"Turn on the CB, Kathy." Dad gave her a gentle push. "Let's find out how much time we have."

"We're really gonna have to leave?" Sarah's eyes widened in fear. "What about Cimmaron, the cows and calves?"

"I'll send Rex to drive them up to the woods."

The static from the CB drowned Dad out. Kathy fiddled with the dials. "*Evacuate immediately!*" suddenly came loud and clear. "The Toutle Valley people must evacuate *now*. Follow the designated roads. Mount St. Helens has erupted. *Evacuate.*"

Sarah turned back to the window. The monstrous clouds hid most of the blackened peak.

Cows and calves milled around the lush spring pasture that stretched to the banks of the Toutle River. She saw Cimmaron trotting restlessly back and forth along the fence. *Maybe I can ride him out*, she thought.

"Dad?" Sarah turned to ask.

"Hurry up, Sarah." Her mother grabbed her arm. "Your father's out in the pickup. We've got to leave right now."

"But, Mom!" Sarah wailed. "What about Cimmaron?"

Mom shook her head. "God will have to take care of him. You can't."

Sarah snatched her jacket off the hook as she and Mom rushed by, then grabbed her boots too.

Out in the yard, Dad whistled Rex off for the cows. At the same time, he opened the gate so the animals could go up in the hills.

Kathy huddled in the rear seat of the king cab pickup, tears slowly trickling down her cheeks.

"My chicks are in the barn," she whimpered.

Sarah gulped and brushed back her hair. She would *not* cry. Crying was for babies. She bit her lip, hard, so she'd have something else to think about. But . . . Cimmaron.

Dad gunned the motor. Gravel spattered as the truck ground up the grade. "Please, God," he prayed. "Get us out of here safely." Then he smiled at his family. "Hang on, everyone. This might be the time we're glad for four-wheel drive."

Sarah knelt on the back seat as she stared back at the farm. Down in the field Rex ran nipping at the reluctant cows' heels, forcing the animals up the hill.

"Dad." Sarah shook her father's shoulder. "Rex isn't getting Cimmaron. He's just bringing up the cows. Please let me go back and get him."

"Sarah . . ."

"But I can ride him up in the hills. We could get to town the back way. I know—"

"Sarah," Dad interrupted her. "No, it's too dangerous. Besides the floods, we don't know what will happen. Maybe the whole area will be buried in ash."

"Dad, please . . ." Sarah's throat choked.

"No, Sarah. You can't go back now."

"Maybe Cimmaron will follow the cows," Mom comforted her daughter. "He hates being alone."

Sarah glared out the back window again. The black pillar had grown until the entire sky seemed alive with ash. Cimmaron stood alone in the pasture, facing the erupting mountain. He snorted and tossed his head. The long mane that Sarah combed every day waved in the breeze. Would she ever feel those driving muscles between her legs again as they cantered across the lowland pastures? Sarah crunched her eyes shut. She would *not* cry. She would prove how responsible she could be.

Kathy sniffled in the other corner. "I didn't get any breakfast."

Once Toutle Farm and Cimmaron were hidden by the trees, Sarah faced the front again and slumped in her seat. She chewed on her lower lip, trying to figure out a way to get back to Cimmaron. Her dad was as bullheaded as they come. Of course, she could take care of herself. She'd been riding since she was four. She knew all the back roads as well as she knew the path to the barn. If only—

"Hang on." Dad's command broke into Sarah's thoughts. He braked hard as the truck rounded the corner. The ancient tan pickup stalled at the side of the road belonged to an old couple who lived above the Sorensons.

"What's wrong?" Dad stepped out of the truck.

The skinny, gray-haired man wiped grimy hands on his well-worn overalls. "I think I got it," he said as he limped back to his door and struggled in.

"What's wrong with your leg?" Mom called out the window.

"Sprained it, I guess." Old Sam shot a gob of brown tobacco at the roadside. He turned the key. The ignition ground and whined. After pumping the gas and grinding some more, Sam banged the steering wheel.

"Old thing never runs when you need it."

"Come with us," Dad invited. "We'll come back for your truck later."

"Ya sure?" Sam asked. "Hate to put you folks out."

Dad snorted. "Put us out? Come on, Edna, you and Sam can ride in front with me. Lizbeth'll get in back with the girls."

A spry little woman, Edna clamped her purse in her gnarled hands as she boosted herself up into the high cab.

"Mornin', Lizbeth, girls," Edna smiled at each of them as she settled herself.

Sarah remembered all the times she had ridden up to Edna's trim white house. The cookie jar was always full and Edna's Jersey cow gave the richest milk in the valley. Sam and Edna had become like grandparents to Kathy and Sarah over the years.

"That old mountain sure changed things around this morning, didn't she?" Edna chirped as Dad slid in beside her.

"Yeah. Don't know the half of it yet." Dad shifted into first gear. "Where you two heading?"

"Just want to get ahead of the flood," Sam answered. "Hope we can come home by tonight. Glad we live up on the hill."

"So are we." Dad clicked on the CB. "Let's find out what's going on."

Mom hugged the girls close. Sarah couldn't believe this. As long as you couldn't see the mountain or the river, everything seemed fine. Just like any other morning when they drove to town.

Sarah glanced at her watch. Sunday school would already be started. Guess they'd miss today. Her first absence this year. *Do you suppose the mountain'd be a good enough excuse? Well, if God really is in control of everything, as Dad keeps saying, then He'd sure better be getting busy.*

Emergency news crackled over the CB. The ranchers talked back and forth, but no one knew what would happen next.

The truck sped around a curve. Sarah could see the eruption again. The ugly, seething clouds had begun to lean toward the east. The mountain and the foothills surrounding it were smothered in dirty gray smoke. The thing had grown and spread, gobbling up everything in its path.

Sarah shuddered. *Would it eat up Toutle Farm too?*

"Easy now." Mom hugged Sarah again. Kathy hid her eyes behind wet fingers. Her sniffing grated on Sarah's nerves.

"Let's pray for our home and your animals," Mom whispered in Sarah's ear.

Whatever good that would do, Sarah thought. *God let that mountain blow. If something happened to Cimmaron—well, God would just have to answer for it.*

All this just proved what Sarah had been burying in the bottom of her mind. *What if God doesn't care? Maybe He doesn't exist. Maybe Mom and Dad are wrong. What if . . . ?*

"Oh, no! Look!" Dad slowed the pickup as it crested the last rise before the bridge. The Toutle River had changed from its milky blue-green, caused by glacier runoff, to a gray, writhing monster. It had long since overflowed its banks and engulfed the lower pasture lands. Trees and bushes twisted and turned as the flood waters tore them out by the roots.

But the bridge still stood. The flood waters hadn't eaten away at the road either.

"Thank You, God," Dad sighed as he eased the truck forward.

CHAPTER 4

As the truck drew closer to the bridge, the roar of the river filled the cab. Kathy stopped whimpering to stare out the window.

Sarah tried to remember the river she'd crossed so often like the deep pool just above the bridge where children swam in the summer. Even on the hottest days the glacier runoff kept the water frigid. The alder trees along the riverbanks leaned over the water, gossiping on the narrow bends. There had been a field with an Appaloosa mare and her colt.

Now the thunder rang in Sarah's ears. The Toutle had gouged out wide banks in its gray, rushing fury. Backwater covered what was left of the field.

Just as the truck crossed the middle of the bridge, an ancient alder tree spun and smashed into the concrete support pillars. The bridge shuddered and bucked like a frenzied horse.

Dad gunned the motor. With a shower of gravel the pickup leaped from the buckling concrete to the stationary asphalt beyond.

Safe on the far side, Sarah looked back, her heart pounding against her ribs. The bridge remained standing. Massive tree roots beat against the pillars. More trees tangled in the turbulence as the high water filled the clearance under the bridge.

"Not sure how long that bridge'll hold." Dad mopped his forehead. "Thank God we made it."

Sarah waited for her heart to quit pounding as loudly as the river. What if the bridge had collapsed while they were on it? She chewed on her lip, thankful for her dad's driving ability. But at that force how long before it reached Cimmaron?

"Dad, what if . . .?"

"Sarah, don't scare yourself with 'what if.' We're safe and that's all that matters."

"But the river must be covering our pasture by now."

"Sarah, I said—" Dad snapped back.

"But Cimmaron . . ."

"Honey." Mom squeezed Sarah's shoulder. "All you can do for Cimmaron right now is pray. God is taking care of us."

"But, Mom . . ."

"You'll just have to trust Him to take care of your horse."

"We'll pray too." Edna patted Sarah's knee.

Sarah nodded. How could she tell them she wasn't sure God really cared? If her own father didn't seem to care, why would God? Yet grownups seemed so sure of Him. Why did she have all these doubts? One of her Bible verses in Sunday school had been about God owning the cattle on a thousand hills. If she could believe that now, maybe the monster gnawing at her stomach would go back in his cave. Sarah gazed unseeing at the REACT—Channel 9 billboards that dotted the roadsides.

As the group approached the town of Toutle, the flashing blue lights of a sheriff's car signaled a roadblock to keep sightseers from sneaking up the valley.

"Mornin', Ted," the deputy shouted above the echoing river. "What shape are the bridges in now?"

"Still standing," Dad replied. "But a tree jam is piling up fast. Could go anytime."

"We've got choppers monitoring the roads and lifting out people in danger. Did you see anyone in trouble?"

"Sam and Edna here." Dad nodded at the old couple beside him. "Their truck stalled close to our place."

"But we didn't go down into the campground," Mom added. "How bad is it further up the river?"

"Don't know, up close to the Red Zone. I overslept this morning. Alarm didn't go off. I was supposed to lead a bunch of property owners in to get stuff from their cabins. They were all lined up at the blockade waitin' for me. Madder'n wet hens."

"I'll bet." Dad shook his head.

"Guess they're pretty grateful now." The man half smiled.

"I'm sure. Anything I can do?"

"Keep your CB on." The deputy pushed his hat back on his head. "The National Guard's been called up. Army Reserves too. They're doing a lot of the rescue work. Settin' up disaster posts. You know," he said, shaking his head, "none of us wanted to believe this would happen."

"I know." Dad nodded. "We didn't either. Even kept putting off packing emergency bags."

"We're asking folks to check in at Toutle High School so we can account for everyone who lives out here. They'll tell you where to go from there."

"Any idea when we can go back? I need to get my animals out if I can."

"Nope. We haven't even seen the beginning of this thing yet. If only people had listened and stayed out of there. We don't know who to look for or where."

"Take care." Dad waved. "And thanks."

Sarah shivered. She'd been so worried about Cimmaron, she hadn't thought about people dying. The farms and houses on the hillsides had been all right as they drove by. All the people were gone. Only the animals remained. And no one seemed worried about all the four-footed creatures.

Sarah glanced at her mother. Mom tried to smile, but fear tightened her mouth. She hid her face against her daughter's blonde head. Sarah leaned against the comforting shoulder. If she closed her eyes she could pretend it was an ordinary Sunday and they were almost to church.

Later after Dad had checked at the high school and discovered they were to go to Cascade Middle School in Longview, Sarah asked, "Did you see Jani there?"

"Nope."

"Well, were the Andersons on the list?"

"Didn't notice. Maybe they'll be at Cascade too."

"But, Dad—"

"You goin' with us, Sam?" Dad cut her off by turning to the old man.

"No, we'll go to Edna's sister's house. Leave more room for those with no folks," Sam answered. "Maybe you can drop us off there."

"You know where they live, down by the Catholic church in Longview?" Edna patted Dad's arm. "Remember the time we had a picnic in their backyard?"

"Yeah, we'll get you there." Dad nodded. "Maybe they'll have the coffee pot on."

"Bet they'll even round up some breakfast, Kathy," Edna said. "You must feel like your backbone's coming through your tummy."

Kathy nodded. A smile trembled at the corners of her mouth. Edna squeezed her arm. "Come on, dear. It'll be all right."

Roadblocks lined the highway all the way down the Interstate 5 freeway. The only vehicles allowed to enter were first aid or rescue and vans belonging to television crews. Everyone else was forced to stop and turn back.

"Please turn on the radio," Mom asked. "That CB is driving me nuts. Maybe the news will tell us more about what's going on."

> Mount St. Helens erupted with the force of an atomic explosion today at 8:32 a.m.

> While ash and steam are drifting east, a 100-foot wall of mud and debris is moving down the Toutle Valley. Spirit Lake is a steaming mass of floating timber. The floods will reach . . .

Sarah couldn't believe it. Spirit Lake? Steaming? What did they mean?

The announcer's voice broke back into her thoughts.

> . . . and the number missing is unknown at this time. Would anyone with information of people on or near Mount St. Helens please notify . . .

"Dear God," Dad breathed. "Please take care of anyone still up there."

"Amen!" Sam shook his head. "I can't believe it. Hundred feet of mud. Old mountaineer Harry Truman musta got his wish."

"You mean to die at his lodge on the mountain?" Mom asked.

"Yep," Sam sighed. "Kinda understand a little. Didn't want to leave our home neither. But no house is worth dying over."

"When you've lived in one place long as we have . . ." Edna blew her nose. Her shoulders sagged.

Later in the afternoon, after a brunch of bacon and waffles, the Sorensons drove over to Cascade Middle School in Longview. Cars lined the streets in the spring sunshine. Daffodils nodded in the slight breeze.

Sarah shuddered at the towering black volcano pictured in her mind. Since the hills hid the mountain, it was hard to believe anything was wrong.

Except for the radio.

Reports of death and damage escalated. Six of the eight bridges had been swept out by noon. The I-5 bridge remained standing but had been damaged. Mudflows from the belching crater turned the Toutle River into a boiling caldron.

Sarah huddled in the corner in the back seat. Each report was more gruesome than the last. Whole families had been swept away. Others, nearer the blast, died in their cars because of the intense heat.

Don't try to tell me there is a God, Sarah thought. *Dad can keep praying all he wants, but I know it's no use. Maybe Cimmaron ran up on the hill—but how far would he have to go to be safe?*

"I want to go home," Kathy mumbled in the front seat. Dad nosed the pickup into the last parking place.

"If we even have a home," Sarah said with a snort.

"Sarah." Mom frowned at her. "You know . . ."

"I don't know anything," Sarah snapped as she slid out the door and ducked under Dad's arm. "And I don't want to hear anymore."

"Sarah . . ." Dad's fingers closed on her arm.

"Just leave me alone! I know we could go back up for the animals."

"Listen to me."

"No way! Look around us! There's nothing wrong. We could go up the back roads!" Sarah's voice grew louder with each word.

"Sarah." Dad gritted his teeth. "You're more important to me than the farm or the animals or—"

"I don't care!" Sarah screamed. "All you ever say is 'God'll take care of us.' " Tears spilled down her cheeks. "I don't believe you anymore. If He really cared, this wouldn't have happened."

"Sarah, I know how you feel . . ."

"No, you don't! You made me leave Cim behind. You . . ."

Dad wrapped his logger-strong arms around her. All of Sarah's fear and anger burst like the top of the mountain. Deep, throat-grating sobs shook her slim shoulders.

Her father let her cry until she hiccupped and wiped her nose.

"Here." He pulled a red print handkerchief from his back pocket.

"Sorry." Sarah mopped her nose and scrubbed at her swollen eyes. Drawing a deep breath, she stuffed the handkerchief back in Dad's lumberjack-plaid jacket.

"Well, let's go." She sniffed. "Storm's over."

Kathy slid from the cab and tucked her hand in Sarah's. Returning her sister's squeeze, Sarah glanced at her mother.

Nodding, Mom wiped her own tears away.

"You girls go ahead," she said. "We'll be right in."

"Sarah! Sarah!" A familiar scream spun Sarah around.

"Jani! You're here!" Sarah dashed across the parking lot. The two friends collided. "When did you get here? Are you okay?"

"Got here last night. Where've you been? They said you were coming here, and I've been waiting forever." Jani tripped over her words in her eagerness.

"Well, we took Sam and Edna to her sister's. They gave us breakfast."

"Sarah, what about Cimmaron?"

"I don't know. Dad wouldn't let me ride him out. We had to leave everything."

"So did we."

The two girls stared into each other's eyes. Then Sarah grabbed Jani's hand.

"Come on, let's see who else is here."

At least I have my best friend, Sarah thought as she and Jani pushed open the doors. *But what will I do if I lose Cimmaron?*

CHAPTER 5

Sarah and Jani froze at the door of the gym.

A bunch of little children screamed and fought over a ball just inside the doorway. Two young mothers tried without success to quiet their crying babies. Two teenage boys passed the time shooting H-O-R-S-E at the basket. A redheaded tease snatched their ball and ran off, both players hot on his heels. Other people milled around as though they were lost.

"We're supposed to stay here?" Sarah questioned.

"Yeah," Jani replied. "The Red Cross brought in cots and blankets. My mom's in the kitchen helping fix dinner."

"Who's in charge?" Dad joined the girls.

"I think that man in red." Jani pointed across the gym. "He was telling people what to do when we got here."

While Dad maneuvered his way across the floor, Sarah said, "Let's find the bathroom. It must be quieter there."

"Down the hall. Come on."

As the door shut, the noise receded to a whisper.

"I've got to get back up to look for Cimmaron," Sarah confided. "Help me think of a way."

"But the mountain is closed off and the river is flooded."

"I know all that stuff. We can't do it today, but we've got to be ready." Sarah chewed on her lip, waiting for an inspiration.

"Is there a radio anywhere?"

"In one of the classrooms. I'll show you." The two girls opened the door, the noise abating as they headed away from the gym.

"In here." Jani and Sarah joined the group sitting near the front where a radio announcer repeated what information they had.

> . . . the first wall of mud has passed under the Interstate-Five bridge and is causing flooding along the Cowlitz River. The rivers are hot to the touch all the way to the Columbia because of the lava and mudflows on the mountain.
>
> Spirit Lake Lodge is buried under 100 feet of mud and ash, and Spirit Lake has been virtually wiped out. The blast, which resembled a gigantic bomb, went north and northeast. Timber was flattened as if a giant laid all the trees side by side, pointing the same direction.
>
> Army Reserve helicopters are searching for survivors in the ash-covered wasteland. The National Guard is assisting in rescue operations.
>
> It is feared that a second wall of mud will travel down the north and south forks of the Toutle before nightfall. Melting snow will increase the flood danger. Ash is falling in eastern Washington, stopping all traffic.
>
> There has been no word from the *National Geographic* team or the *Columbian* reporter, Reid Blackburn. At this time the death toll is unknown but may reach more than a hundred.
>
> This is . . .

In the late evening, after a cafeteria-style dinner, and the cots and blankets had been doled out to the families, Dad gathered his family for devotions.

"Here?" Sarah burst out, her eyes wide.

"Of course."

"But we don't have a Bible."

"I have plenty stored here." Dad tapped his forehead. "That's why God has us memorize His Word. Then we can use it when there's no Bible around."

"Oh." Sarah huddled on her cot. She hoped no one was listening. You could hear everything each family was doing, with all the cots side by side.

"In the Old Testament," Dad began, "God says, 'Call upon me in the time of trouble and I will deliver you.' "

Sarah wished her father would speak more softly. It seemed that he wanted everyone around them to know about their devotions. Some things should just be personal. What if the kids teased her tomorrow?

"Sarah, are you listening?"

"Umm."

"Then what's your answer?"

Sarah stared at her fingers in her lap. The middle one had a long hangnail.

"Could you repeat the question?" she muttered.

"Sarah." Mom leaned forward. "Do you feel embarrassed?"

"Uh-huh."

"Honey," Mom whispered and patted Sarah's clenched fists. "We believe God is taking care of us, and we want to share Him with everyone. Our family devotions are a way of sharing. Maybe a family right over there really needs to hear God's promises tonight."

"I suppose so," Sarah agreed, "but, Mom . . ."

"Let's pray." Dad glanced at each member of his family. "Father, thank You for caring for us. Thank You for . . ."

Sarah's mind raced off like a hound after a rabbit. *Why do you say thank you when your very, very best friend is missing? Where was Cim? Was he safe under the trees or . . . Why won't Dad at least listen to me?*

"Your turn." Kathy bumped Sarah's arm.

"Please let me go look for Cimmaron tomorrow, amen."

"Help us to claim Your promises for our own," Dad finished, "and thank You most of all for Your Son, Jesus Christ, amen."

"Tomorrow we'll buy some underwear and pajamas," Mom whispered as she tucked each of the girls into her cot.

"Good. Sleeping in my jeans is icky," Kathy whispered back.

"Sure wish that baby would quit crying," Sarah muttered with a groan.

"He'll settle down as soon as it's quiet," Mom answered. "Babies don't like their schedules upset. They like their own beds even more than we do."

The high gym windows were lightening to gray when Sarah awoke to the sound of the wailing baby again. At least he had slept most of the night. She jumped out of her warm cot and slid her feet into her waiting boots. Sleeping in your clothes sure made getting dressed easy. She combed her rumpled hair back with her fingers, then tiptoed to the hall. Both Dad's and Mom's cots were empty. Kathy snored on. The smell of early-morning coffee told Sarah the adults had already gathered in the kitchen.

> . . . the interstate bridge over the Toutle River is still standing but closed until its safety is assured . . .

The radio announcer's voice greeted her ears as Sarah opened the kitchen door. Several men with steaming cups of coffee and two teenage boys surrounded Dad in the corner.

"That means we have to go clear out to the coast and around by Raymond," Sarah heard one man say.

She eased over to the corner and perched on the edge of a table.

"Well, we've gotta salvage what we can *now*, in case that mud dam breaks," another insisted.

"Let's have some breakfast first." Dad nodded to each of the men. "Maybe by then the patrol will let us cross the bridge."

"Yeah, if we can get to Vader, we can go in on the back roads."

"At least there's no ash down around our area," another added. "But if the wind turns . . ."

"Yeah, eastern Washington and points east got that. Can you believe, volcanic ash a foot deep in Ritzville? They're having more problems right now than we are." The men ambled over to stand in line for scrambled eggs and toast. Sarah followed. She was going to be ready when they were. Somehow she had to convince her dad to take her along.

The men were finishing their second cups of coffee when a state trooper approached their tables.

"Mornin', folks," the trooper said. "I've got good news for you. The I-5 bridge is still officially closed, but we'll let you cross, one at a time. That way you can go back up the river to check on your homes and livestock."

"How long will we have?" Dad became the official spokesman for the group.

"You'll have to make it fast. The National Guard out of Toledo will be helping you."

"Thanks." Dad patted the man on the shoulder as he went by. "You going home soon? You look beat."

"Who knows?" the officer responded, shaking his head.

"Dad." Sarah trotted to keep up.

"Not now, Sarah."

"But, Dad, I can help. Please—may I go?"

"That's crazy! You stay here with your mother and Kathy."

"But those boys are going. You know how good I am with animals. They calm down for me. Besides, I can drive the truck too."

Dad paused outside the door. He saw the other men taking their sons. He stared into Sarah's tense blue eyes.

"Dad, please!" Sarah shoved her hands deep in her pockets. *He had to let her go!* Cimmaron was up there. He needed her. She stared back, trying to answer the question in her dad's eyes.

"I can do it," she whispered.

"I know—you're tough." Dad shrugged. "Go tell your mother where we're going."

Sarah darted back through the door. While she wanted to scream the news, she ran silently down the hall to the kitchen.

"Dad said I could go along. Back up the river."

"Sarah, you can't do that. It's too dangerous."

"Dad said I could."

"He must be crazy," Mom muttered under her breath. "You be careful." She shook her head again. "God be with you."

"Oh, *Mother!*" Sarah waved as she dashed out the door.

The line of rescue vehicles had grown to thirty or more before the red pickup approached the bridge. Flashing blue lights indicated the roadblock. Since the northbound lanes of the two parallel bridges had taken the brunt of the flooding, the troopers motioned the slow-moving line across the grass in the median. One at a time, the trucks cautiously crawled across the southbound span, crossed the median again, and sped up the freeway. As Dad and Sarah took their turn, Sarah stared at what had been a small, peaceful river valley.

Solid, silver-gray mud filled in the valley, forcing the Toutle River to cut new channels, as the still-hot water raged its way to the Columbia River. The campground had disappeared under forty feet of mud, the slime marking the high-water level on the trees left standing on the hillsides. The tops of alder trees dotted the gray plain; the mangled body of a blue Volkswagen Bug perched like a new kind of bird's nest in the branches of one tree. The river cut its way around house-sized boulders that had tumbled along with the flood.

Sarah scooted closer to her father. Neither could say a word. The gray scene was too awesome.

Truckers and their eighteen-wheelers clogged the southbound lanes of the freeway, patiently waiting for the bridge to reopen. Some of the truckers waved to the passing drivers. The CB crackled with their comments and guesses as to what would happen next.

As soon as the truck crossed the hill, Sarah marveled. Nothing was changed. The alder trees showed new green fuzz among the firs and hemlocks. Only the two-lane line of truckers was out of the ordinary.

Dad turned off at the Toledo exit, following the line of cars and trucks in front of him. One by one, the patrolman at the roadblock waved them through.

"Keep your CB on," the patrolman reminded. "If we holler 'Get out', you drop whatever you've got and *get out!*"

"Thanks." Dad waved in acknowledgment.

Dad drove swiftly up the hills and around the curves until he and Sarah could see the valley again. A barn roof and silo top resting on the mud sea were mute evidence of a once prosperous farm. The location of the house was marked by a mercury yard light on a tilted pole.

In the low places, silver ash-mud hid the road. Dad shifted into four-wheel drive. The truck rumbled along with ease. Where the mud had dried, it looked like concrete.

A helicopter clacked overhead, then crow-hopped up the valley.

Sarah switched on the radio.

. . . up to one hundred persons feared dead. Rescue attempts are continuing. At this time the mud dam at the south end of the devastated Spirit Lake is holding, but the water is building up behind it.

"Dad, you have to let me ride Cim out. He won't make it if that water bursts."

"It's too dangerous, Sarah. But if we find him, perhaps we can drive him high up into the woods or lead him out."

Sarah knew this would have to do. "Thank you."

"I'm not promising."

"I know." She crossed her fingers so hard they hurt.

CHAPTER 6

Sarah huddled next to her father as the pickup plowed through areas of gritty mud on the road, then sped up when the way was clear again. She couldn't believe her eyes. The once lush, green Toutle Valley was a solid sea of gray mud. Farms had disappeared. Only hillside houses remained, the rest buried in the muck. The remaining once-tall trees looked like squatty bushes dotting the moonscape.

Several army trucks and local pickups nearly blocked the road as Dad and Sarah crossed the next hill.

"What's happening?" Dad asked as he braked his truck.

A mud-covered man in drab green answered, "Animals caught in the mud. We're draggin' 'em out."

Sarah jumped from the truck as Dad parked behind the others.

"Hurry, Dad!" she called over her shoulder.

Ahead, three men worked over a bedraggled animal on the ground. Two other cows stood spraddle-legged, with heads hanging. Mud still dripped off their steaming bodies.

Dad caught up with Sarah to join the men hovering over the fallen cow. The animal lay on the ground, ribs heaving with deep, struggling breaths.

"Not sure about this one," one of the men said. "She was in pretty deep." He carefully felt the cow's ribs. "Can't feel any broken on this side."

"Can we leave her alone for a while?" someone asked.

"No, better try to roll her up. She'll get pneumonia lying there."

The men struggled with the cow. One pulled on her head while Dad and an old farmer tucked her legs under her. Sarah knelt by the animal's ribs and push-lifted on the resisting back. Slowly the cow rolled up to rest on her folded legs. She coughed, then dropped her chin on the ground. Sarah stood up and braced her knees into the animal's back to keep her from rolling back. The cow coughed again, shaking her head.

"She's looking better." Sarah rubbed the muddy neck. "Come on, girl. You can do it."

"Let's get 'er all the way up," one of the guardsmen encouraged as he slapped the gunky animal on the rump.

Sarah bounced her knees into the cow's back.

"Come on! Do it!"

The cow shook her head resentfully.

"Get up! You can make it!"

The cow's chin balanced on the ground; her hind feet struggled for footing. The men braced her on both sides as she straightened her front legs and stood panting. Sarah beamed at the men and the cow. They'd done it!

Crack! A rifle shot echoed across the valley. Sarah's heart leaped like a deer during hunting season.

"What're they doing?"

"An animal was still alive but too far gone to pull out," one of the soldiers answered. "Can't leave 'em to suffer, so . . ."

Nausea churned in Sarah's throat. They couldn't just shoot one of the cows. As if the animals hadn't been through enough. Couldn't they have tried harder? A large, muddy hand on her shoulder interrupted her runaway horror.

"It's the only way." Dad's voice seemed far away.

Sarah nodded, then rubbed the cow in front of her.

"At least we saved these." Sarah swallowed hard.

A tall blond man hauled a bale of hay from the back of a truck and broke it on the ground in front of the wary cows.

"That'll hold 'em 'til they're picked up. Let's head up the road. There may be more."

Sarah raced for their truck. They had to hurry. Maybe Cimmaron was caught in the muck like that. She'd never let anyone destroy him. They had to pull him out! No matter what! Cimmaron *must* live. She'd pull him through.

Led by the pickup, the caravan of rescue vehicles ground over the next hill. At the edge of the gray mud wash, the blacktop disappeared. On the far side, the road completed its journey over a new hill. The mud looked like a dense fog had drifted across the hollow. Even in four-wheel drive the truck wheels slithered and spun, unable to keep their traction.

Dad rocked the vehicle back and forth, then reversed and backed out onto the solid road.

"Stuff's too deep. Not solid enough to drive on yet."

"Any way we can get around this?" The officer in charge approached Dad's window.

"Yeah, back a ways is a loggin' road," said Dad. "Get turned around. I'll show you."

One by one, the trucks turned in the narrow road and followed the red pickup about a quarter of a mile back to where a log barred the way on a right-hand turnoff. Two army men jumped out of the back of their canvas-covered truck and heaved the log off to one side. Sarah grinned and waved as Dad shifted back into four-wheel drive. The caravan bumped up the hill. The radio crackled as Sarah punched buttons, trying to zero in on the local station.

. . . the mud fill at the south end of Spirit Lake is still holding. This is KBB in Longview . . .

"Turn the CB up, Sarah. That was the news we needed to hear."

The caravan reached the main road again without incident. Sarah wished for wings on the truck. They were almost to Toutle Farm. And Cimmaron would come out with them.

"Would ya get a load of that," Sarah breathed as the truck crested the last rise.

White-faced cows and calves calmly grazed on the grass along the road. A muddy but ecstatic cow dog barked madly as soon as he recognized the truck. As Sarah threw open the door, Rex leaped to the floor and then to the seat. His entire body, from nose to tail, was one huge wag as he covered Sarah's face with slurpy kisses. After greeting Sarah, he turned to Dad.

"He sure earned his nickname this time." Sarah giggled. "Ol' fastest tongue in the West." She wiped her cheeks, then hid her face as Rex's tongue reached to kiss her again.

"Good boy. Down!" Dad fended off the joy-crazed animal as Sarah jumped from the cab.

"Come on, Rex." Sarah dashed to the top of the rise. She whistled, then listened intently. No answering whinny.

Sarah whistled again, but only a bawling cow answered. Below her, several animals caught in the mudflow had quit struggling. A hungry calf trotted back and forth at the mud's edge, crying for his trapped mother. The cow mooed in a frenzy, frantic because she could move only her head.

A whine at her knee drew Sarah's horrified gaze from the cow.

"Where is he, Rex?" Sarah knelt and, holding the faithful dog's head between her hands, looked in his eyes. "Where's Cimmaron?"

Rex whined again, then flicked a kiss on her nose. Sarah hugged him close.

"Oh, where is he?" she whispered in the dog's fluffy ears.

Sarah stood up. She sucked in as much air as her lungs could hold. Her two-toned whistle for Cimmaron echoed across the wasteland.

Nothing. No whinny heralded the arrival of her red-gold horse. No tossing head with pricked ears. No twitching whiskers nuzzling for grain. Just gray muck and bawling cows.

But I prayed, Sarah thought. *I asked and God didn't answer. Guess that proves it. He really doesn't care.*

"Sarah, God does care." Dad nodded seriously as he reached her side. "He does."

There he goes again, Sarah thought. *Reading my mind. Please let him be right.*

"Maybe Cimmaron went up over the hills," Dad offered.

"Maybe. I'm not gonna give up." Sarah clenched her fists. *Even if God isn't real, I'll find Cimmaron,* she promised herself.

"Right now, let's get those cows out. There's more up here!" Dad yelled. "Bring ropes and slings."

Praying is crazy if God isn't real. Sarah's mind tumbled on. *But somebody has to help me. I can't do it all myself.* Sarah shook her head. At least she could help with the cows. She recognized Sunshine, mired more deeply than the others. But where was her calf?

Slowly the rescuers slogged across the mud to the trapped cows. Using small army shovels, they dug carefully around the nearest animal. With mud up only to her belly, it didn't take long to dig a trench to free her legs. Sarah slipped a makeshift halter on the cow's head.

"Come on, old girl," she crooned. Dad pulled on the rope and one of the soldiers pushed from the rear. With a bellow, the cow lurched forward.

"Here, girl. Let's go."

The cow slipped and fell to her knees. While Sarah pulled on the halter, Dad and the men boosted from the rear.

"Come on, girl. Your calf's waiting." As Sarah talked encouragingly to the cow, the men hoisted and slipped until they pulled the animal free.

All the while, the calf trotted around at the mud's edge, bellowing for his mother.

"Think you're about starved to death, don't ya?" Sarah chuckled as the calf made a beeline for his mother's udder. Once the rope was removed, the cow nuzzled her baby and began grazing at the roadside.

Sarah gave the reunited pair a last pat and trudged over to where the men were digging Sunshine free.

"She's in pretty deep." The old farmer shook his head.

"But we saved that other cow," Sarah reminded him.

"Yeah, but . . ."

"Dad, have you seen Sunshine's calf?"

"Uh, no."

Sunshine lay with her head on the mud, too tired to even flick her ears when Sarah patted her.

"Come on, Sunshine, you gotta try." Sarah sat down in the slop, hoisted the cow's head, and slid so her legs held the animal's head out of the mud. "Easy now. You're gonna make it. You've got that beautiful baby to feed," Sarah murmured on, comforting the cow.

The men dug down on both sides of the cow, then tunneled under her behind her front legs. As soon as there was space, they threaded the sling and ropes under the cow. By the time the process had been repeated in front of the back legs, everyone looked like abominable mud men.

"She's a heavy one," one of the guardsmen muttered. "It's going to take all of us."

"Sarah, get a rope on her head," Dad panted. Sarah knotted the sludgy rope around Sunshine's neck, and then slipped a noose over the apathetic nose.

"All together now!" The men grabbed the ropes and heaved. Dad glanced at Sarah, talking the animal free. If anyone could make the animal want to live, Sarah could.

The men strained again. The cow moaned, then struggled. One more desperate heave and Sunshine lay gasping on her side—free. Dad stared at a patch of muddy red hair at one side of the gaping hole. Carefully he dug a bit more. The small red calf stood entombed in the mud. Dad stopped to wipe moisture from his face.

"Dad, what is it?" Sarah ran back to his side. Her eyes followed her father's. With a cry, she dropped into the hole and dug frantically around the still body.

"It's no use, Sarah. He's been dead since the mudflow."

Sarah flung herself into her father's arms.

"But he's so little," she sobbed. Dad patted her back, his own tears making gullies in the mud on his face.

"I know. I know. Life isn't always fair."

"I hate it! I hate it!" Sarah screamed into his shoulder.

"I know, Sarah, I know. But sometimes we have to just live through it."

But I don't want to live through it, Sarah thought. *I want things back the way they were. I want Cimmaron.*

CHAPTER 7

Dad held Sarah close until her jerky sobs quieted to shivers.

"I—I'll find him," Sarah finally sniffed. "S-s-somewhere Cimmaron is still alive." *I'll find him*, she promised herself.

"I hope and pray so." Dad gripped Sarah's shoulder and turned toward the road. "You OK now?"

Sarah barely nodded.

"Then why don't we take care of Sunshine?"

With the slings still around the cow, two rescuers had dragged her across the mud. The thin layer of water on top greased the way.

Sunshine was lying alongside the road, but had already rolled up on her folded legs. After giving the cow a rub behind the ears, Sarah pulled on the rope. Dad slapped the cow on the rump, then steadied her as she grunted to her feet. Sunshine rested for a moment before she staggered to a large clump of grass. Instantly, the grass disappeared down her throat.

"She'll be OK," Dad nodded. "Rex." He waved the dog toward the cows.

Rex sniffed Sunshine's nose, then flopped down in a patch of grass.

"You gonna let her rest before you round 'em up?" Sarah ruffled the dog's ears. The *fastest tongue* washed the remaining tears from her cheeks.

"We can leave your cows some hay and come back for them later," the officer in charge said as the men climbed in the trucks.

"No, I'll get 'em rounded up and move them into our land across the road. It's up in the timberland and fenced, so it should be safe from any flooding."

"You need some hay for them?"

"Yeah, thanks. There's not much grass."

The men quickly transferred four bales to the red truck.

"Need any help?"

"No, thanks. We got 'er."

With a wave, the officer climbed aboard one of the mottled green-and-brown one-ton trucks.

"Be sure to listen to your radio!" he yelled back.

As the rumble of the trucks disappeared over the hill, Sarah took a deep breath and rotated her shoulders.

The glorious scents of spring had been buried in the gray ash. The air smelled of mud and sulphur smoke.

"Let's hustle, Sarah. You and Rex bring the cows. I'll drive ahead to open the gate and kick out the hay."

"Come on, Rex. Get the cows." The dog loped back over the rise to round up the stragglers. As soon as the truck passed them, Sarah slapped the cow nearest her on the rump and waved her arms.

"Let's go, you guys. Move it!"

Sarah dreaded seeing the farm as she and the cows topped the hill. If she just watched the animals—didn't look. Instead she stopped to inspect every inch of gray ooze, in case Cimmaron's red body was trapped out there.

"He's not there," Dad shouted. "At least I didn't see him anywhere."

As the last cow ran through the gate with Rex nipping at her heels, the CB blared into life.

"Get out! Everybody out! The dam is going!"

Dad slammed the bar on the metal gate. "Let's get outa here. Come on, Rex." He waved at the dog.

As Sarah stepped up into the truck, she glanced up the lane to her father. Dad frantically waved his arms, trying to regain his balance, as a large rock turned and sent a small avalanche of rocks rattling into the ditch. His fall seemed to be in slow motion, but instead of getting up and jumping in the truck, he lay there. Not moving. Not talking. One leg twisted under the other.

Oh, no! Not him too! Sarah's mind screamed as she leaped from the truck and ran to her father's side.

"Dad! Dad!" She knelt at his head. His dark lashes looked extra-long as they lay on the pain-blanched cheeks. Sarah tried to remember what she'd learned in 4-H about first aid. His eyes blinked open.

"Musta slipped, huh?"

"Sure did. Can you move? Your leg looks bad, may be broken."

"Feels like my head is too."

The CB blared on. "Get out! Everybody out!"

Sarah felt Rex's nose nuzzle under her arm.

"Dad! We've gotta get outa here!" Sarah shrieked in terror.

"Sit up. Can you move?"

Groggily, Dad raised up on his elbows. He stared at the twisted leg.

"We better get me in the truck before the pain hits. Hefting me is going to be worse than lifting those cows."

"I'll back the truck up here. We can slide you in the back." Sarah muttered her thoughts aloud. "Please—hang on!" She nearly screamed again as his eyes closed.

"Don't worry." Dad groaned. "Just resting."

Sarah crossed the road and jumped into the truck in two bounds. Still in a haze, she started the engine and backed the truck into the lane. *This can't be happening*, she thought.

"Hang on, Dad. Hang on."

Sarah knelt on the rocks beside him. "Here, give me your arm. We'll hoist at the same time."

He nearly fainted as the two of them stumbled to their feet. His right leg straightened with a grinding crunch.

"Don't stand on it." Sarah staggered as his heavy body sagged against her.

Dad shook his head, clenching his teeth to keep from screaming.

The two steps to the lowered tailgate seemed miles away. By the time Sarah pulled and pushed Dad down the length of the truck bed to lean against the cab, sweat was pouring off both their faces.

"I'll get some hay to brace your leg." Sarah leaped from the truck bed and clambered over the gate where the cows calmly munched the alfalfa. She grabbed several large hunks and threw them ahead of her over the fence. Dad barely nodded as she packed the hay around his swiftly-ballooning leg.

"Rex, up here." In an instant the dog jumped up and snuggled next to Dad. "Keep Dad warm. Stay." Sarah slammed the tailgate shut and climbed back in the cab.

"Oh, God," she prayed, "get us back to town—please!"

Glancing over her shoulder to make sure her father hadn't fallen over, Sarah shifted the truck into four-wheel drive and started the long drive for help. She tried to avoid all the holes, but every bump felt like a canyon. Sarah stopped the truck as they reached the detour into the logging road.

"Lay me down," Dad moaned when Sarah touched his shoulder. She heard his leg grind again as she helped him lie down. With the hay packed around his leg again, she lifted his head and gave him some extra hay for a pillow. Then she took off her jacket and tucked it around his still body. Rex snuggled back down beside Dad's arm.

"Good dog," Sarah whispered as she started the truck up the rough hill. Logging roads weren't built for comfort or speed. She'd have to stay in four-wheel drive.

"Don't think about the flooding," Sarah reminded herself as the blaring CB intruded on her concentration. *At least I know all the roads if we have to take to the hills. I've ridden over every one of them with Cimmaron. Will we ever ride like that again?* Sarah shook her head. *Can't think about that either. Hope Dad is unconscious—then he won't feel all the ruts.*

With a sigh of relief, Sarah reached Spirit Lake Highway again. So far—no flooding. The mud-packed valley looked the same as it had this morning. She shifted gears into first, then second and third as the asphalt road dipped and rose smoothly in front of her.

"Breaker, breaker, this is Sarah Sorenson." She pushed the *send* button on the CB speaker, then released it.

"Go ahead, Sarah."

"I'm just turning onto 505 from the Spirit Lake Highway, heading toward Toledo. My dad's in the back. He fell, and he broke his leg."

"We'll have an ambulance waiting at the roadblock. Can we do anything else?"

"What about the dam?"

"Still seeping. Get out as fast as you can."

"10–4." Sarah hung the speaker back on the set. Tension crept up over her scalp as though her mother had braided her hair too tightly.

Sarah was afraid to drive too fast. Her white knuckles, clenching the steering wheel, made it easy to oversteer. "Smooth it down," she told herself. "No bumps." She rolled down the window so she could hear her dad if he needed her.

"You guys OK back there?"

Rex's whine was her only answer.

The blinking lights at the roadblock ahead signaled help; someone else would be taking over. Sarah slowed the truck, trying to keep from jolting. As soon as it stopped, one of the sheriff's deputies climbed in the back with a first-aid pack.

"Hey, young lady," the deputy shouted. "Help me with this dog."

Sarah shook herself free of the numbness creeping up on her and slid out of the truck. In the rear Rex still lay by his master's side. Growling and baring his teeth, the dog dared anyone to approach.

"Rex, you fool dog." Sarah rubbed his ears. "It's OK. They're not gonna hurt him."

With a whimper Rex snuggled under her arm, all the while keeping a wary eye on the officer.

Dad groaned. He blinked and tried to focus on the man bending over him.

"Sarah?"

"Right here, Dad." Sarah reached for his hand.

"Thanks."

Blinking hard, Sarah watched as the officers strapped a splint along Dad's leg, then carefully lifted him onto the stretcher.

"Hit his head too, did he?"

Sarah turned to the man beside her. "Yeah, when he slipped. Knocked him out."

"Was he unconscious long?"

"About a minute."

"We're taking him to the hospital in Longview. Where's your mother?"

"She's at Cascade School in Longview." Sarah answered the questions with only part of her brain. Seeing her father placed into the ambulance made her numb. Nothing could happen to her dad. He never got sick. All those years logging, he never got more than a cut or two.

"I'm always careful," Sarah could remember him saying. "And you know, God takes good care of me."

"Well, He sure blew it this time," Sarah muttered under her breath.

"What's that?" the man asked.

"Nothing." Sarah started at the question. They'd think something was wrong with her too, if she wasn't careful.

"We'll follow the ambulance," the deputy said. "I'll drive your truck for you. We've radioed for your mother to meet us at the hospital."

Sarah nodded as she climbed back in the cab. Rex jumped in right beside her. Flashing red lights and a screaming siren led the way.

CHAPTER 8

Sarah sat in a daze during the trip to Longview. Since the I-5 bridge had opened, traffic was moving freely. The officer, driving the Sorensons' truck, made no attempt to keep up with the wailing ambulance.

Sarah answered the man's tentative questions with yes or no; her mind couldn't think any further. Even though the heater was going full blast, shivers chased each other up her back and along her arms.

"Here, take my coat." The officer shrugged out of his jacket as they stopped at a traffic light. Sarah wrapped the jacket around her shoulders gratefully, but the shaking wouldn't stop.

"Hey, your dad's going to be all right."

Sarah only nodded. Sensing her fear, Rex nosed her ear and whined for attention. Absent-mindedly, Sarah scratched his ears.

"Stay," Sarah commanded as the truck pulled into the parking lot of the aging brick hospital. Rex dropped to the floor and rested his chin on the seat.

"You can't come!" Sarah ignored the pleading in the blue eyes.

"This way." The officer touched her arm and pointed to the emergency entrance.

Inside, the antiseptic smell made Sarah wrinkle her nose. A nurse showed her to the cubicle where the doctor was clipping open Dad's pant leg. Her mother turned to greet her.

"Oh, Mom." Sarah buried her face in her mother's comforting arms. "I was so scared."

"Me too. But he's going to be fine," Mom murmured, stroking back Sarah's tumbled hair. "Hush now. You were great."

"It was such a freaky accident."

"I know. You can tell me all about it later."

"Mrs. Sorenson," the doctor interrupted, "we'll be taking your husband to surgery right away. I've called. The orthopedic specialist is on his way."

"Thank you."

"You can wait upstairs. It'll be several hours before you'll be able to see him again."

Sarah glanced at her watch. Three o'clock. Getting up this morning in the gym seemed like days ago. It was as though it had happened to someone else.

"You're sure there's nothing I can do?"

"No, your husband is already sedated. We're getting the best orthopedic doctor around."

"We'll go get Sarah something to eat, and I'll be back shortly."

Two nurses in baggy green cotton pants and shirts, with round caps covering their hair, pushed in a narrow, rolling table with a thin mattress on it. Deftly, they transferred Dad from the examining table to the gurney. His eyelids fluttered as Mom kissed him on the forehead.

"Love you," he whispered.

Sarah tried to smile and say something as Dad's cart rolled by her but the lump in her throat made talking impossible. Instead, she squeezed his hand, then clamped her lower lip between her teeth. *You will not cry! If you start you'll never stop. Have to stay strong to get Cim.*

All those years logging and he'd never even sprained an ankle. What was God thinking of to let her father get hurt like this? And if He didn't help Dad who believed in Him, why should He help Cimmaron?

Wait a minute, Sarah told herself. *No God, remember?* Since God didn't exist, she couldn't pray or—but it was natural to talk with Him, to expect Him to care. What a muddle!

"Coming, Sarah?" Mom broke in on her thoughts.

"Yeah. Yeah, sure." Sarah shook her aching head. That's all she needed. A headache!

"You all right?" Concern wrinkled her mother's forehead.

"My head just hurts."

"You haven't eaten, that'll do it. Let's go somewhere quiet."

Later at the restaurant next door, between bites of fried chicken and mashed potatoes, Sarah told her mother all about rescuing the cows, Dad's fall, and the long drive back to town.

"But we didn't see Cimmaron anywhere," Sarah stressed. "I've got to go back and find him."

"Sarah," Mom said as she handed her a napkin, "you can't go up there again. In the first place, you have no way to get there, and in the second, you'll have to take care of Kathy. I'll be spending most of my time at the hospital. Your father needs me 'cause he won't make a very good patient."

"But . . ."

"No, Sarah. I can't worry about you off in the woods right now. And besides, the valley is closed again."

Sarah stared at the chicken bones on her plate. Stay at the shelter? How useless.

"Sarah, are you listening?"

Sarah nodded. "May I go back to the hospital with you?"

"No, I'll drop you off at the school. You can shower and change clothes. Kathy and I went shopping this morning, so you'll have something clean to put on."

Sarah looked down at her mud-caked shirt and jeans. She'd forgotten all about them. She must look as bad as the cows she had helped drag out.

"Mom, what about Rex?"

"Oh." Mom paused. "I know. I'll take him to Sam. They have a fenced-in yard there."

Back at the school, Sarah spent the next hour explaining all that had happened to Jani, Kathy, and a group of wide-eyed youngsters. They clustered around her like chickens at feeding time, hanging on her every word. She carefully skipped the part about Sunshine's calf. She'd leave that until Kathy asked. Kathy cried a little when Sarah told of the accident.

"Dad's going to be all right," Sarah assured her. "The doctor promised."

"I gotta get a shower," Sarah said finally. "You guys go play. Come on, Jani. Keep me company."

"Your clothes are in that bag on your cot," Kathy pointed out. "We bought toothbrushes and stuff too."

"Shampoo?"

"Yeah. And use the school's towels. That's what we did this morning." Kathy trotted off to join her new friends while Sarah and Jani headed for the shower.

"Did you *really* drive that far?" Jani asked in amazement.

"I was scared to pieces, Jani. What if my father was dying? His face was as white as—as your T-shirt. And then I heard that bone grinding in his leg when we got him in the truck." Sarah shuddered, then continued shedding her clothes behind the cubicle curtain.

"I could never do all that." Jani shook her head.

"Never thought I would either." Sarah stepped under the steaming spray. "But no sign of Cimmaron anywhere. I called and whistled 'til I couldn't pucker, but . . ."

"What're you gonna do?" Jani raised her voice so Sarah could hear her.

"Go back and look for him some more."

"How?"

"Dunno. I'll find a way."

"What about . . ." Jani paused.

"About what?" Sarah had tucked a towel around herself, and rubbed her wet head with another. "Man, that felt good. Now, what?"

"Your dad's pickup."

"Mom's got it."

"I know. But later."

"I don't know, Jani. If I get caught, Mom and Dad will kill me."

"Maybe catch a ride with the others when they go back in?"

"Maybe. No, they'd insist on getting Mom's okay."

"Which she won't give with your dad in the hospital," Jani sighed.

"Well, keep thinking."

Later that evening, when Mom returned from the hospital, she tucked each of the girls into bed with a special hug.

"Your dad's going to be OK," Mom whispered. "It was a bad break, so he'll be in the hospital for a few days. They can't put the cast on until the swelling goes down."

"What about his head?" Sarah asked.

"Not serious. He'll be dizzy for a while."

Sarah let out a deep breath. What a relief! She had been imagining all kinds of bad things. She'd never been around anyone hurt that badly before.

"Now, let's pray together for him." Mom bowed her head. "Heavenly Father, thank You that Ted's not worse. Please heal his leg quickly."

"Take care of my father and . . ." Sarah felt as if she were being pulled in two directions. How could she pray to a God she wasn't sure was real? She wanted to do what her mother said, but she felt like a phony.

After the amens, Sarah lay on her cot trying to figure things out. All the death on the mountain—people, livestock, wild animals, even the trees and flowers. Sunshine's calf. She could feel the tears behind her eyes again. *No! Not Cimmaron. He's still alive—somewhere.*

Wednesday crept by. Sarah and Kathy remained at the shelter. They couldn't even go to the hospital. The rule said no one under fourteen could visit the patients.

But the evening become a buzz of noise when they heard President Carter would visit the next day. It kept everyone awake late that night.

"Aren't you excited?" Jani poked her friend.

"I guess. But, Jani, this place is driving me nuts. All I can think about is Cim."

"Well, I don't know about you, Sarah Sorenson, but *I* want to see the president. *In person!*"

"OK, OK. Don't get uptight. I want to see him too."

The crowds began gathering at the school early in the morning. By noon there was standing room only.

As a cavalcade of cars approached the school, the television crews pushed in front of the spectators. Sarah watched from a tabletop as security men, dressed in raincoats and three-piece suits, formed two lines from the long black car to the gym. President Carter stepped from his limousine and waved.

Looks just like on television, Sarah thought. After shaking the outstretched hands and speaking briefly to the adults in the room, President Carter made his way to a little girl huddled on a cot in the corner. Kathy had been going over to talk to her each day. Her parents had been killed on the mountain.

Television cameras rolled as the president squatted in front of the child, who had her face in a blanket.

"Ah'm sorry about your mommy and daddy," he drawled, then turned and looked Kathy right in the eye.

"Hi," she whispered shyly.

"Hi, yourself," he said, shaking her hand. "You bein' taken good care of here?"

Kathy nodded, then stared around the crowd for Sarah.

The president answered some questions from the crowd.

"It's hard to believe what happened on that mountain," he said into a microphone. "I'm still in a state of shock." Then he smiled and waved again as he climbed back in the waiting car.

Jani danced Kathy around in a circle. "You actually touched the president," Jani chanted. "He's almost as good as a movie star."

Sarah tried to join in the fun but she kept looking back to the little girl. Both of her parents—dead. No more family—no home—nothing. Those people who died had families who had to go on living without them, and some of those families were kids just like her and Kathy. At least their dad would be coming home.

Sarah wandered through the thinning crowd to where the little girl still hunched on the cot.

"Hi." Sad, big, dark eyes stared up as Sarah sat down.

"My name's Sarah. What's yours?"

"Kim."

"Umm, I heard about your . . ." Sarah chewed on her lip. *What do you say when something like this happens?* "Uh. Sorry. Don't even know what to say."

Kim nodded. One tear rolled down her thin cheeks. Her eyes looked like rain-filled pools, ready to overflow.

"Do you know what'll happen to you next?"

"She'll go to a foster home," said the woman who was watching Kim.

An idea jiggled in the back of Sarah's brain. Maybe they could fit one more in at their house. Dad always said, "Share." Well . . . she'd better talk to her mom this evening.

"We'll see, Kim." Sarah smiled. "We'll see."

CHAPTER 9

"Sounds like you had an exciting day." Mom joined the girls on their cots that evening. Kathy had finally settled down after shaking hands with the president. She'd been bragging all afternoon. Everyone was aware of her "celebrity" status.

"Sarah. Looks to me like you've got something on your mind again."

"Yeah. Mom, I've been thinking. You know how you always tell us to share?"

"Yes."

"Well, you know that little girl who was on TV? Her name's Kim? Both her parents died in the eruption."

Mom nodded.

"Now she doesn't have any family—not even people she knows, 'cause they just moved here. So I just thought—well." Sarah stuttered. "Well what do *you* think?"

"Sure I feel sorry for her, Sarah. But what are you getting at?"

"Well, umm—I think she should come live with us."

Kathy jumped up again. "Oh, yes."

Mom stared at Sarah.

"Mom, you said we should help others whenever we can and share . . ."

"I know what I said, Sarah. Give me time to think. This is a big decision."

"I thought maybe I could make a bedroom downstairs, next to the family room. Kim could move in with Kathy."

"Slow down. Easy. Let me talk it over with your father."

"But, Mom, do *you* want her?"

Mom studied Sarah's face. She knew it was set in what her parents called her stubborn look, but she was tired of them ignoring her ideas. Maybe she could at least save this girl. Or try.

Mom nodded. "Yes, Sarah, I want her. We've plenty of love for one more. But it's not that easy."

"Oh, Mom." Sarah beamed.

"Now hang on. First I want to talk with your father and Kim too. Then we have to work with Social Services."

"But we're going to try?"

"We'll see. That's the best I can say right now. And it's nice to see you thinking about someone else."

That night Sarah had a hard time going to sleep again even without the baby crying. She pictured the new room—all by herself. She could put her bed in the corner, and her dresser would make sort of a wall—and that old frame could be covered for a screen. In a room all by herself. That sure would be different.

What kind of sister would Kim be? Probably bratty at times like Kathy. But how much more terrible to no longer have parents.

"We'll see," Mom had said. *Well,* Sarah thought with a smile, *with my mother* we'll see *usually means yes. Unless Dad says no.* Sarah frowned. *But he keeps saying God will take care of us. So how's God going to take care of Kim without our help?*

Friday and Saturday dragged so slowly that a snail race would have been exciting. Dad had agreed with Mom—they could make room for one more. Now it was in the hands of the social worker. So far, no one had claimed Kim. It seemed she was indeed an orphan. After getting permission from the woman who was watching Kim, Sarah and Kathy moved the little girl's few belongings to Dad's cot.

"You may sleep by me," Kathy promised.

Sunday morning Mom attended church with the three girls before she went to the hospital. It seemed strange to Sarah not to hear her father's deep voice singing the hymns. Kim sat between Kathy and Mom, amazement widening her eyes.

"Never been to church before," Kim whispered.

Sarah's eyebrows disappeared into her hairline. "I thought everybody went to church." Mom shook her head.

That afternoon, when Sarah talked to her dad on the phone, there wasn't much to say. What could she say about the center? *We watched television, read a book, played basketball*—how boring! Besides that, she couldn't tell him about her *big* project—finding a way to look for Cimmaron.

Everyday she and Jani dreamed up new plans to get the horse back. Somehow there had to be a way. "Never give up" was their motto.

Monday morning, the world was light gray. The trees, cars, everything wore ash frosting. Ash sifted under the doors and clung to shoes and coats. Sarah made a beeline for the television room.

. . . the winds shifted, blowing from the northeast. The heaviest ash fall was in the Kelso-Longview area, and as far north as Centralia, then south over Portland. Stay off the roads. If you have to be outside, wear a mask or cloth over your nose and mouth.

Sarah raced frantically to the school kitchen, where Mom was stirring the oatmeal.

"Mom, have you heard the latest reports?"

"Umm." Mom added some salt to her kettle. "Here, honey, you set the milk and sugar out."

"But—but Cimmaron won't be able to breathe in that ash either."

"I'm sorry, but there's nothing I can do about it."

Sarah glared at her mother. "I don't think you care anymore."

"Oh, Sarah, of course I care. There's just nothing I can do."
Mom dished up two bowls of oatmeal. "Come on, let's eat."

"But, Mom!" Sarah felt like shaking her. "This *is* an emergency. Cimmaron needs me."

Mom put down her spoon. "Now listen to me." Her eyes grew stern. "And listen to me good. I know you want your horse back. I understand how you feel, but I will not put you or myself or anyone else in danger to find him. Is that clear? It's a gift that your dad is okay."

Sarah gritted her teeth. Her mother didn't get upset very often, but when she did. . . .

"I s'pose so," Sarah mumbled.

"I do have an idea though," Mom continued. "Why don't you call the animal shelters to find out if someone has seen him? I heard a man talking about that yesterday. People are bringing the animals they save to the shelters. Folks can claim them there."

Sarah brightened at the suggestion. She'd thought animal shelters were just for stray dogs and cats. What if . . .? She gobbled up her cereal.

"I'll get you change for the phone before I leave for the hospital. Oh, and the Red Cross brought masks for us. Put one on if you go outside."

Sarah and Jani spent the next couple of hours calling the animal shelters. Jani was the very best friend she could have, Sarah thought. When Jani's voice got hoarse she'd drink some water and keep on calling. Each one would give them the number of another. But the answer was always the same. No bright sorrel gelding with a white blaze.

One place had two goats, some sheep, a donkey, and a small herd of Angus cows. There was a pinto mare and a bay gelding at another. The shelters were begging for all kinds of animal feed from alfalfa to birdseed.

"Well, at least they promised to keep an eye out for him," Jani tried to comfort Sarah.

"Yeah. They said they'd call me." Sarah's voice trailed off. The two girls hunched under the wall phone. Discouragement oozed from every pore.

"Wanna play Old Maid?" Kathy and Kim stopped in front of Sarah and Jani. Kim had officially declared herself Kathy's shadow.

"Nope."

"You're supposed to help entertain us. Mom said."

"Take a flying leap . . ." Sarah stopped herself. If Kathy tattled? "I'll play later. Right now I've got some more figuring to do."

Kathy shrugged. "That's what you always say." She and Kim scrambled off when Sarah's glare melted their socks.

By Tuesday morning, Sarah was a wreck. She had hoped the ash would disappear like a bad dream, but the world was still gray. A breeze created small tornadoes in the parking lot.

"I have a ride down to the hospital again," Mom informed the girls at breakfast. "I'd hate to take the truck out in this."

Sarah stopped eating. An idea whirled in her brain like the ash twisters outside. The truck would be here! The spare key was stuck under the glove compartment. She and Jani could drive the truck up to look for Cimmaron, and if they hurried, they'd be back before anyone was the wiser. Mom usually stayed at the hospital until evening. There was no one to stop them.

"Now, make sure you take care of the younger ones." Mom patted Sarah's shoulder. "Maybe when I get back tonight we can watch a movie."

"Sure, Mom." Sarah could hardly contain her impatience.

"Bring us something?" Kathy hinted.

"We'll see." Ash powdered the floor as Mom opened the door. "Be good now." With a wave she climbed into the waiting car.

Sarah dashed down the hall. Jani was in her usual chair in front of the television.

"Come on, lazy bones. Big plans." Sarah jerked Jani to her feet.

"What are ya doin'? I want to watch TV."

"I don't care! Come on!"

Jani's eyes widened as Sarah dragged her down the hall-way. "What are you doing?" Her screech could be heard clear to the gym.

"We're going after Cimmaron."

"Now?"

"Yes. Grab your jacket. Mom left the truck here."

"Sarah, you said before you couldn't drive it again."

"But now it's an emergency with this ash. We'll be back before anyone knows we left." Sarah spoke firmly to quiet the little voice yammering in her brain. Little "what if" just had to be quiet. She could do it. They had to find Cimmaron.

After locating the key and starting the truck, Sarah backed it up and drove slowly out of the schoolyard. Once the pickup entered the main street, Sarah found that the ash had been scraped to the side. Traffic was light but moved slowly. Sarah braked and shifted cautiously at the stoplights.

"Good job," Jani cheered, waving her water bottle as the girls crossed the bridge into Kelso.

"Yeah, it's the freeway next. If we make it to Vader all right, then it'll be easy."

"What about the roadblocks?"

"We'll take all the back roads. They can't block 'em all." Sarah tried to be nonchalant as the red truck picked up speed. At least traffic wasn't moving at its usual sixty miles per hour. The draft from the semis billowed clouds of ash up from the sides of the pavement, making it hard to see. Sarah's fingers ached from clenching the wheel. The twenty miles passed slowly. *This is taking all morning*, Sarah thought. With a sigh of relief, she signaled to turn off the freeway.

"We made it." Jani slumped against the seat. She coughed a little and sipped at her water.

"Didn't see one patrolman. Lucky!"

As the girls drove east, paralleling the Toutle, they found the ash had drifted deeper than it had in town. Sarah drove slowly to keep the stuff from blowing higher than the truck.

"Shame we can't go in on 505."

Sarah shook her head. "That's where the roadblocks would be. I want to get as close to home as possible. Thought we'd take those logging roads on the ridge behind our house. If he didn't go down the river, that's most likely where he'd be."

"Maybe Cimmaron came back to join your cows."

"Maybe. That would sure make it easy." *Wouldn't that be great*, Sarah thought. *If I could see him, know he's safe. Then I could put up with anything. This not knowing is driving me crazy.*

But when Sarah parked the truck below the gate at the hillside cow pasture, there was no answering whinny to her whistle. The cows, huddled under the trees, bellowed at her as if asking for something to eat that wasn't covered with gritty gray stuff. Only Cimmaron wasn't there to blow in her face and nuzzle in her pocket. Would she ever play "which hand" with him again?

CHAPTER 10

"Do you think Cimmaron might have headed over to our place? He really likes our horses," Jani said.

Sarah jumped back in the truck. "Good idea. If we can get through. I haven't driven on the road any further than this."

"Oh!" Jani pounded on the dashboard moments later. Another mudflow blocked the road. The Andersons' drive was further up the hill.

"I don't dare try to get through that," Sarah said glumly. "We'd get stuck for sure."

"Wish I could see what's happened to our house. It's on the hillside but . . ."

"Let's walk it."

"I dunno . . . I'm scared."

"Why?"

"Well, you know, the house, the animals. Who knows what it'll be like?"

"I'll try whistling from here. If Cimmaron is at your house, he'll hear me."

Sarah's whistle brought no response, except from a big black crow high in the fir tree. Every time Sarah whistled, the crow cawed. Sarah glared up at him as she climbed back in the truck.

"Dumb bird."

"At least there's something still alive around here." Jani motioned out at the gray wilderness.

"Yeah, I know." Sarah backed the truck until she found a turnaround. "Well, guess we head for the logging roads. What time is it? I forgot to put my watch on this morning."

"Almost eleven. We better hustle."

The logging roads were like a maze; one led off from another. The ash lay deeper along the ridges. Everywhere it billowed around the moving truck like a desert dust storm. Jani and Sarah wore the same gray garment as the truck. Jani started coughing harder.

"Ugh! I keep chewing on this stupid ash," Jani muttered.

"My throat's sore," Sarah coughed. "It's getting harder and harder to whistle."

"Want a sip?"

"No, you need it more than me."

"Any idea where we are?"

"Sorta."

Jani glanced at her watch again. "It's getting close to three."

"Just one more road, then I'll turn back."

"Your mom . . ."

"I know! But maybe Cimmaron is up here somewhere, hurt. I have to find him."

"He coulda gone further down the river instead."

"Umm, could be."

Sarah's eyes ached from peering through the dust. Every time she rubbed them, it felt like rocks grinding in her eyelashes.

Just then the engine coughed and sputtered. She glanced at her gas gauge. It still showed almost a quarter of a tank, so that couldn't be the problem. The engine barked once more; then there was silence. Sarah shifted into neutral and turned the key. The starter whined, but the engine refused to turn over. Sarah pumped the gas and ground the ignition again. More silence.

"What's wrong?" Jani eyes showed white against her gray skin. Her voice sounded hoarse.

"I dunno. There's gas enough. Maybe if we let it rest for a bit."

"OK. But boy, the water's gone and am I thirsty."

"Me too."

Sarah leaned against the door and shut her aching eyes. A sigh that came clear from her toes started her coughing again. She stared at Jani. They both sensed a little ghost of fear riding the dust motes around in the cab.

"There's always the CB," Sarah said to reassure both of them.

"Yeah, try the engine again."

Sarah turned the key and ground the ignition for a few seconds. She released the key and tried again. The grinding filled the cab for several minutes, then faltered.

"Now what?" Jani whispered.

"I don't know. Let's wait a bit." Seconds passed like creeping snails. Sarah turned the key again. The red light on the gauges blinked once and went out. The turning key clicked, then was silent.

The ghost of fear grew solid. Sarah could see it mirrored in Jani's eyes. She felt a tightening in her shoulders.

"Breaker, breaker, this is Sarah Sorenson." She released the call button. No answer.

"Breaker, breaker, this is Sarah Sorenson. Do you read me?" The CB remained silent. Sarah shook the speaker, then checked to make sure it was attached to the set.

"Breaker, breaker." A cough caught in Sarah's throat. "Please, do you read me?" Slowly she hung up the speaker.

"Let it rest too?" Jani tried to smile.

"Yeah, everything's tired around here," Sarah tried to joke. Neither of them laughed.

Sarah opened the door and stepped outside. A breeze blew up ash puffs that matched the clouds scuttling across the tops of the ridges. Gray ash blowing off the trees blurred the lines between sky and ground. *What are we gonna do?* Sarah wondered.

"Bet it's the battery." She slammed the door, causing a gray dust storm in the truck.

"Can we do anything?"

"Try again. If rest is gonna do it . . ." Sarah turned the key. The light flickered; the ignition growled and clicked.

"What about the CB?" Jani's voice almost disappeared.

"Breaker, breaker." Sarah knew before she spoke that it was dead. "It runs off the battery too."

"You're right. I forgot."

"Someone'll find us." Sarah zipped up her jacket. The late afternoon chill crept into the cab.

"No heater either?" Jani questioned hopefully.

Sarah glared at her.

"Dumb question, huh?"

Silence prevailed except for a brief rain shower that spattered on the roof, then moved up the hills.

"If we're going to start walking, we better get going before dark," Jani said finally.

"No way!" Sarah shook her head. "Dad said if I was ever lost, to stay in one place until someone found me."

"But we're not lost. We can follow the logging roads downhill 'til we get to the main road."

"Do you know how long that would take us?"

"Not really."

"Do you know where we are?"

"Not for sure."

"Well."

"But we gotta *do something.*"

"Yeah, we are. We're staying right here. Besides, there's no way we'll have enough breath to walk."

Jani sulked in her corner for a few minutes, then said, "When do you suppose they'll start looking for us?"

"Who knows. What time is it?"

"Four-thirty."

"Let's see. My mom usually gets back from the hospital about five. What was your mom going to do today?"

"Going somewhere, but she'd be back at the school by now to start dinner."

"Kathy and Kim would have missed us hours ago. People could be looking already." Hope lightened Sarah's fears.

"But how'll they know where to look?"

"Got me." *Dad'd tell me to pray in a mess like this*, Sarah thought, *but I got into this by myself. Guess I'll have to get out of it any way I can.*

"What if the mountain blows again?" Jani's whisper sounded loud in the silence.

"Don't be dumb."

"But it could happen."

"I know. Lots of things could happen, but I'm not gonna think about them." Sarah chewed her lip. The gritty ash reminded her how long it had been since breakfast. *Don't think about food either*, she ordered herself.

Jani opened her door. "Br-r-r." She shivered as she scrambled back in the cab. "That wind cuts right through you."

The whirling ash from the open door sent Sarah into another coughing attack. This time she coughed until her chest ached.

"You OK?" Jani patted Sarah's shoulder.

"Yeah, as long as I don't breathe." Sarah grimaced.

"Funny. That's my line."

"Yeah." Sarah took small breaths. Deep ones not only made her cough but also stabbed through her chest like daggers. Her throat was as raw as her eyes.

Dusk crept up on the girls. The clouds hid the sun, so darkness came early. The gray faded to black until the trees were only a darker outline.

"Guess nobody'll find us tonight," Jani whispered.

"Probably not."

"We could sing all the songs we know. That'd pass the time," Jani said after awhile.

"Sure, if my throat didn't hurt so bad. Doesn't yours?"

"Yeah. Another dumb idea."

"What about ghost stories?"

Jani looked at her friend. "You gotta be kidding. I'm shaking in my shoes already."

Sarah started to laugh but hacked instead. "What time is it?"

"Oh, sure. I'm supposed to read my watch in the dark?"

"Maybe there's a flashlight in the glove compartment. Dad keeps one in each car."

After fumbling with the catch, the girls felt everything in the compartment carefully. Pens, paper, even a plastic ketchup container from a drive-through, but no flashlight.

"How about under the seat?" Sarah dropped to the floor on her knees. She found some tools, a paper cup, and gloves, which she handed up to Jani. "And a flashlight," she sighed with relief as she pushed the switch. Ash danced in the light. Sarah shone the beam up on Jani. White teeth and eyes gleamed out of her ash-covered face.

"Jani! You look awful!"

"Thanks. You're not so hot yourself."

"Don't make me laugh," Sarah pleaded as she shone the light around the cab. They had reason to laugh now, she thought. How come such a simple thing as a flashlight made such a difference? She even felt warmer because of the light.

"Crazy." Sarah shook her head.

"Sarah, we can use the flashlight to signal if we hear anyone."

"Then we'd better save it." Sarah clicked it off. The darkness was even blacker now that the light was turned off. Slowly the girls' eyes adjusted again.

The girls listened carefully for a long time. All they heard was the wind crying in the trees.

"We have to breathe quieter," Jani said finally.

"Sure, you tell the wind that too."

"Shine the light here so I can see the time."

Sarah flicked on the light and shone the beam on Jani's watch. Ten o'clock. It felt like midnight or later. Time sure was creeping along.

Sarah turned the light off and laid it up on the dash. She shoved her hands in her pockets and tucked her legs under her, then snuggled closer to Jani.

"You cold?"

"No, just freezing." The two huddled closer together. Soon the wind moaned to deaf ears as sleep claimed them.

Chapter 11

Sarah woke sometime during the night with a cramp in her leg. As she jerked her leg straight, Jani woke and stared around.

"What's wrong?" Jani mumbled.

"Got a cramp," Sarah answered, rubbing her muscle vigorously.

"Turn on the light. Let's see what time it is." Sarah fumbled for the flashlight. Her cold fingers didn't want to push the button.

"Three."

"Is that all?" Sarah rubbed her arms and legs to get some circulation back in them. "Maybe we'll be warmer if we lie down on the seat."

The two snuggled down again. Sarah had her back to the rear of the seat and held Jani's shivering body against hers. She could hear a rasp in Jani's throat. Pillowing her head on her right arm, Sarah drifted off. *God, please make them find us, please don't let anything bad happen to Jani,* she prayed before sleep claimed her.

Sarah woke the next time to the cawing of a crow and the faraway clack of a helicopter. She blinked at the sunshine pouring in the window. The sun glinted off the minute glass particles in the powdery ash. With the wind gone—stillness.

The clack was coming closer.

"Jani." Sarah shook her sleeping friend.

"Umm," Jani mumbled.

"It's a helicopter."

"You sure?"

Sarah stared at Jani. Her voice could barely be heard and she had a feverish look in her eyes.

The clack-clack of the blades was definitely nearer. Sarah leaped from the truck.

"*Help!*" she screamed, jumping up and down, arms flailing like windmills. "Here we are! *Help!*"

The chopper hovered above the treetops. "Get back in your truck and roll up the windows," boomed down at the girls from a bullhorn. "We'll try to set down in the road ahead of you."

Sarah scrambled to obey.

Jani lifted her head a little but weakly fell back on the seat.

Sarah clung to the steering wheel. She could hardly sit still. "Quicker, quicker," she muttered. She reached out to hold Jani's hand.

"Someone found us," Sarah whispered past the lump in her throat. "They found us."

Great clouds of ash rose above the trees and enveloped the truck as the whirlybird settled on the road. With a final clack, the long blades of the green chopper stopped. Quiet settled along with the dust.

Sarah doubled over with another coughing spasm.

"You OK?" Jani wheezed.

"That hollering sure does it," Sarah nodded in return. Each breath hissed in and out of her ash-tortured lungs. "All that dust must be why we had to get back in the truck."

"Uh-huh."

Just then, two men loomed out of the settling ash. White masks hid the lower part of their faces.

"You girls all right?" the man at Sarah's door asked.

Sarah nodded, afraid to speak in case she started coughing again. The other man opened Jani's door.

"What were you doing out here?" the same man asked.

"Looking for my horse," Sarah croaked past her raw throat. "The truck stalled. Jani needs a doctor. I think her asthma is bad again."

"Well, let me tell you, you have some worried parents. They figured you'd be up here somewhere."

"Did you run out of gas?" his partner asked.

"No, there's almost a quarter of a tank left."

"Bet it's the air filter then," the two men nodded. "This ash clogs 'em up real quick. Plays havoc with the engines."

Sarah clutched the steering wheel tighter. Boy, were she and Jani in for it! She'd never planned for any of this to happen. Driving up here to look for Cimmaron had seemed so simple yesterday. She could just hear her dad. "All you ever think about is that horse. When are you going to grow up? Think of someone else for a change?" Sarah shuddered. Her deep sigh exploded in wrenching coughs. And she wasn't as bad as Jani.

"Come on, kids." The officer opened Sarah's door. "Let's get you out of here. Bet you'd like a drink of water too."

"What about my pickup?"

"They'll send a tow truck after it when they can. Maybe just put in a new air filter." Two white gauze masks with elastic strings dangled from his finger.

Sarah swallowed slowly. The water cooled her parched throat.

The pilot flipped some switches after hooking his safety harness in place. The water felt so good, Sarah didn't even pay attention as he talked over the radio. Maybe she'd be able to talk better now.

"Thanks," Sarah said gratefully, as she drank some more, then handed the canteen back to the man in front. She slipped the elastic string over her head and snapped the mask in place. She wrinkled her nose, trying to get the mask comfortable. Jani's eyes closed again. Sarah reached over to put the mask on her. A heavy stone feeling sat in her stomach. *Please, God, help Jani.*

"Here we go, kids." The pilot revved the engine, and with a loud clatter the rotor blades spun into a blur. Dust filled the copter as it lifted straight off the ground.

Sarah looked at Jani. Her eyes were scrunched shut; her hands clutched the seat in front of her.

Sarah wiped away a tear and tried to watch for Cimmaron.

"What does your horse look like?" one of the men yelled above the noisy engine.

Sarah grimaced as she described Cimmaron.

"Haven't noticed one like that," the men agreed. "And we've covered a lot of ground this week."

Sarah marveled at the view. The ridges, some studded with evergreens, others logged bald, rolled away beneath them. Mount St. Helens, still belching steam from her cratered peak, loomed to the east.

"Toledo coming up." The pilot pointed ahead.

As the helicopter hovered above the ground, Sarah could see Jani's parents and her mother waiting by the cars. A light from an ambulance came closer towards them.

Jani grabbed Sarah's hand. "Not your fault."

Sarah nodded. *But it was*, she thought. Her shoulders hunched up to her ears. If only she could make herself invisible. Then no one could lecture her. How stupid they'd been, taking the truck out like that. Her dad was right. Sometimes she didn't think. And now Jani was sick. Sarah's guilty thoughts beat in her brain. If only—if only—kept time with the slowing of the chopper blades.

"Unbuckle your seat belts, ladies." The pilot turned and smiled at the girls. "We made it."

The ambulance attendants carried Jani to the stretcher. With dragging feet, Sarah crossed the grass.

"Sarah, you scared me to death. Are you all right?" Mom asked, putting her hands on Sarah's shoulders.

Numbly Sarah nodded. "But the truck isn't. It quit on us."

"Oh, Sarah!" Mom wrapped her arms around her daughter. "I've been praying and praying. I tried not to worry—I just—oh, thank God you're safe." Mom dug in her pocket for a hanky. "Thank You, Jesus, for keeping my girl safe," she whispered again.

Sarah felt safe, huddled in the circle of her mother's arms. *What if it was God watching out for her?* She had prayed. *Maybe . . .*

Sarah glanced at her mother. The set of her mouth promised more to come.

"We'll watch for your horse," the pilot assured Sarah after the thank-yous and good-byes had been said. "Keep your chin up."

"Come on, Sarah," Mom said as she waved good-by. "We'll drive the Anderson's car to see the doctor. After the doctor gives you a good going over, we'll go see your father."

"But the hospital won't let me see him."

"He'll be coming downstairs to the waiting room in a wheelchair."

"Oh." Sarah no longer felt safe and secure. Now she'd *really* get it. "He's pretty mad, huh?"

"Wouldn't you be?"

"Prob'ly." Sarah chewed her lip again.

"You know, Sarah, your father and I, we trusted you."

"But Cimmaron . . ."

"And you disobeyed. Now listen to me and listen carefully." Mom grasped one of Sarah's hands. "You not only put yourself and Jani in a terrible situation that could have cost you your lives, but you also endangered those who had to come after you. Unnecessary rescues from the ash are costing a lot of time and money. You added to the problem."

Sarah stared at her grubby hands. She couldn't look her mother in eye. Why didn't Mom get mad and scream? Get it over with. Even a spanking would be better than this.

At the doctor's office, Sarah remembered what her mother had said. "You added to the problem." What was her father going to do?

When the doctor ordered her to breathe deeply, Sarah coughed until her head swam. Even her ears hurt. The doctor listened carefully to her lungs and heart.

"I think you'll feel a hundred percent better after a shower," the doctor said to Sarah. "The warm steam will make it easier to breathe. Generally, you're okay. The coughing is a direct result of the ash. It will take time for your lungs to heal," he continued, putting his stethoscope back in his pocket. "I'll give you a prescription for some cough medicine. Sucking on cough drops will ease your throat. If your cough doesn't quit by next Monday, or you start running a fever, call me."

The doctor stopped at the door. "You can be grateful, Sarah. There are others lots worse off than you."

Sarah nodded as she buttoned her shirt up again. Tears dripped down her cheek. Others like Jani.

"Thank you for seeing us so quickly," Mom said as the three walked down the hall.

"You're sure welcome," the doctor replied. "And Sarah, stay out of the ash."

"I will. Is Jani going to be okay?"

"It will take a while before we know. She inhaled all that ash, and it's not good for her lungs."

Once out in the cold air again, Sarah bent double with a coughing spasm. "Now what?" she asked when she could talk again.

"First, we'll get you some breakfast. Then I'll turn your prescription in to the hospital pharmacy, so they can fill it while we talk to your father. We'll get some lozenges at the same time."

All too soon, Sarah tried to disappear in a chair as a nurse wheeled her father into the room. The silence after the nurse left smashed her into the chair. Sarah felt like a mouse in a corner, waiting for the cat to pounce. She sucked on her cough drop. *Why doesn't he say something?* her mind screamed.

Unable to stand the tension any longer, Sarah peeked at her father through her eyelashes. Dad slumped in the wheelchair several feet in front of her, his thick white cast from thigh to toes extended in front of him. His blue eyes looked so sad that Sarah studied her hands again.

"Well?" Dad asked softly.

Sarah wished she were anywhere but here.

"Sarah, look at me."

Inch by inch, Sarah raised her eyes to the buttonholes on his pajama top.

"Sarah . . ."

She took a deep breath, coughed, and glared straight at him. "I had to find Cimmaron!"

Dad shook his head. "It could have cost your life or someone else's."

"But Jani will be okay."

"Sarah."

"I know. I'm selfish and only think of myself or my horse."

"Well?" Dad's eyebrows raised.

"But, Dad, Cimmaron needs me too. If he's still alive." Sarah paused. "What are you going to do?"

"I'm not sure. Your mother and I have been praying for wisdom ever since we heard you were safe. Before that, we prayed that God would protect you. And He did."

Sarah chewed on her lip. She saw Mom at the window across the room, her head bowed, most likely still praying.

"I think," Dad continued after another long silence, "that you will have to pay for the truck repairs and the towing bills, if there are any. Then, if they send us a rescue bill, you'll have to pay as much of that as you have left in your savings."

Sarah melted further into the chair. She'd worked hard for her money, odd jobs wherever she could. Baby-sitting, cleaning house for a neighbor, washing windows for another and more baby-sitting. She had been working and saving for over a year for a new saddle. She glanced up at her father to find a look of such disappointment on his face that she wanted only to throw herself into his arms.

"I—I didn't mean to. I mean, all I wanted was to find Cimmaron." Tears burned her eyes.

"I know. But part of growing up is learning to figure out the consequences of your actions—before you do something. And now you have to earn back our trust too. Trust is a really hard thing to re-establish." He sighed. "And Sarah, your mother and I love you so much . . ."

All that, the ash, the truck, Jani hurt, she thought, *and I never even saw Cimmaron. What if something really terrible had happened?* The drumming of her heart filled the silence of the room. "What do I have to do—to get your trust back again?" Her words caught on the lump in her throat. *Please, Dad, don't hate me.*

"I don't know at this point, but we'll talk about it some more. I hope and pray that what you've been through has taught you a lesson." He shook his head slowly, all the while those eyes staring right into her. "You see, God did take care of you. Do you have anything more to say?"

Sarah shook her head, but the words screaming in her mind whispered out. *I'm sorry, I'm so sorry.*

CHAPTER 12

Sunday morning dawned with promise for the Sorensons. "We're going home today," Mom whispered as she woke each of the girls. "We'll pick up your father at the hospital right after breakfast and go home."

Go home. Going home. What wonderful words. Sarah rejoiced as she pulled on her jeans.

"Oh, boy," Kathy bubbled. "Hey, Kim, wait 'til you see my new calf. He was born the day before the mountain blew."

Sarah stared at her mother. In all the hullabaloo she'd forgotten that Kathy didn't know her calf had died. Sarah's eyebrows flagged the question. *Later*, her mother mouthed as she shook her head.

"If he was a heifer," Kathy tripped on, "I'd name him Helen, but since he's a bull—what do you think, Sarah? What would be a good name?"

"You could name him Black Cloud," Kim suggested. "Or Blacky."

"Blacky!" Kathy hooted. "He's a red Hereford with a white face."

Kim giggled in return. "Then how about Reddy?"

The two giggled at each of the names they dreamed up as they trotted off to the bathroom.

"What are we going to do?" Sarah helped her mother fold their clothes.

"I suppose waiting's made it worse. She hasn't asked about him, so I guess I hoped she'd kind of—well—forgotten."

"You have to tell her before we get home."

"Umm." Mom brushed her hair back with the back of her hand. "I'll do it right after breakfast. Get washed and we'll eat."

Later, after the family finished eating and the repaired truck was loaded with their belongings, Sarah looked around the gym once more. Nearly all the evacuees had gone home or found other places to stay. With the cots put away, the gym looked large and ready for school. *Sure won't miss this place,* Sarah thought. *Even going to school would be better than staying here. Funny, we came here a four-person family and are leaving with five people. At least for now,* she amended. *Wonder if we'll get to keep Kim?*

"Why don't you and Kim sit in the back?" Mom said when Sarah opened the truck door. Before turning the ignition key, Mom took a deep breath and put her arm around her bouncing younger daughter.

"Kathy, I have some bad news for you," Mom said, brown eyes gazing into brown. "Sunshine's calf died in the flood. When your dad and Sarah pulled Sunshine out of the mud, her baby was already dead."

"Oh! But, Mom!" Kathy wailed, throwing herself against her mother. Her sobs ricocheted off the doors. Sarah tried to swallow past the lump in her own throat. She knew how Kathy felt. For sure, it wasn't fair. With a shiver, Kim pressed her tiny body up against Sarah's side. Sarah put her arm around the little girl and held her close until Kathy's crying turned to sniffles.

"I'm really sorry, Kathy." Sarah patted the trembling shoulder in the front seat.

"I know losing anything you love is hard." Mom blew her nose. "But I thank God you are all safe. That's the most important thing to me. Now." She started the truck. "Let's get your dad and go home."

Several hours later, after checking Dad out of the hospital and picking up Rex, the Sorensons pulled into their own driveway. Mom parked the truck next to the ash-frosted Pinto and they all stared across the farm.

The mudflows had reached only a couple of inches on the basement of the house. The barn was buried up to the eaves. The hipped roof rested on mud-concrete. A person could step from the ground right up into the haymow.

"Well," Dad quipped after a deep sigh, "that'll make it easier to get the hay out."

Sarah tried to smile at her father's attempt at humor but all she could think of was Cimmaron. If only he were here too, then she could be grateful for what they had left.

Dad carefully maneuvered his crutches up the stairs to the front of the house. As the family went through the door, the crackle of the CB met them.

"At least we have electricity." Mom smiled. "Do you suppose that thing has been going all this time?"

"No," Dad replied as he sank onto a kitchen chair. "They just got the electricity back in here a day or two ago. That and my leg are why we didn't come back sooner."

"Come on, Kim. I'll show you our bedroom." The two younger girls scampered down the hall.

"Well, our first job is to get that pickup unloaded. Then you can take some hay up to the cows." Dad nodded at Sarah. "Looks like that ash-mud is solid as stone. Kathy can help you carry the bales to the truck."

"While you girls do that, I think I'd better start on the refrigerator." Mom gave the appliance a dirty look. "Bet that'll smell *bad*."

The stench of rotten meat nearly knocked everyone over when Mom opened the freezer compartment.

"Quick, Sarah, get a trash bag," Mom muttered, trying not to breathe. "We'll just dump everything in it and tie it up outside."

Sarah gagged as she held the green plastic open. Abruptly, she dropped the edges and rushed out the door. The sound of her retching penetrated to the kitchen. Mom dumped the rest of the food in the bag and quickly carried it outside.

Sarah leaned over the iron railing. "Sorry," she moaned as her mother came back up the steps.

"You OK now?"

"I'll live."

"The bad news is we still have the downstairs freezer to do. I'm glad it was close to empty. Though how we'll ever get that stink out, I don't know."

They walked back into the kitchen, arm in arm, in time to hear Kathy's horrified, "Pee-yuu! What stinks?" She and Kim huddled in the hallway, fingers pinching their noses shut.

Dad snorted, then chuckled. Holding out his arms to his wife, he shook with laughter. Sarah couldn't see much to laugh about, but Dad's chortling was contagious.

"Pee-yuu," Dad howled, with his fingers over his own nose.

What a crazy bunch we are, Sarah thought when she could breathe again from laughing hard enough to crack her ribs.

"Laughed so hard I almost fell over." Mom wiped her eyes.

Kathy's "Oh, Mother," set them off again.

Rex barked and scratched at the door. "Let him in. He wants in on the fun." Dad waved toward the door.

"Oh, my." Mom gave Dad one last hug. "Guess I better open some canned food for dinner. Bet you're all hungry."

"Come on, Kathy. Kim, you can help too." Sarah grabbed her jacket off the hook and headed for the door. "We've gotta unload the truck, then feed the cows."

"Where are they?" Kathy asked.

"Up across the road. Let's go."

That afternoon Dad called Sarah into the living room where he had mail scattered all around him, on the sofa, the floor, and the end table. He held up two bills, then handed them to her. "I'm sorry to have to do this but—you remember our discussion when they brought you back in the helicopter?"

Sarah nodded. Her shoulders slumped with her sigh. *I hoped you had forgotten.*

But he hadn't.

She took the statements and after swallowing, followed the numbers down until she saw the total on the first page. Truck repairs: $290.86. She glanced at her father who was watching her.

"Actually, that's cheap considering what they had to do."

"Oh." She flipped to the second page. The towing bill: $120.00. Sarah chewed on her bottom lip. $410.86. Her shoulders lifted again in a sigh. "I-I'll take the money out of my account tomorrow if Mom can take me to the bank." *Goodbye, saddle. But then, I don't have a horse anyway, so what difference does it make?* That left her with $156.00. If a bill came from the rescue she'd be flat broke. Could the money help buy trust back?

"You can be grateful the National Guard didn't send us a bill for rescuing you." He took the papers she handed back to him. "At least not yet."

"Yeah." Sarah sniffed and turned to leave. Somehow right now being grateful for anything at all seemed about as hard as putting the top back on Mount St. Helens. If she ever did get Cimmaron back, she'd have to ride bareback. Her old saddle lay entombed in the mud-filled barn.

By Monday morning Mom and the girls had the house cleaned and some baking done. They still struggled with the odor in the freezers. Dad spent most of his time lying on the sofa, keeping his leg up like the doctor ordered.

"Sarah and I are going to town for groceries," Mom announced at the breakfast table. "Kathy, you and Kim entertain your father." Mom smiled across the table. "There's soup for lunch. Kathy, you may bake some brownies. The mix is in the cupboard."

"Bring me back some books from the library," Dad requested. "Sitting around like this is driving me crazy already."

"Mom," Sarah asked, once they were on the road, "can we go to some shelters and look for Cimmaron? Maybe come home along the river?"

"Yes to the first question, no to the second. While I get the groceries, you can call all the shelters from the pay phone. Something else I've been thinking. Why not run an ad in the paper? Then if anyone has seen him, they can let you know."

"But how? We don't have a phone yet."

"Give 'em an address. They can always write."

"Thanks, Mom. Do you have any change?"

"We'll get some."

"No luck, huh?" Mom said as she came out of the grocery store.

"Nope. Lots of animals, several sorrel horses even, but none of them match Cimmaron's description. They said they'd get a hold of me."

Mom nodded sympathetically.

"Mom, what am I gonna do? How can I look for him?"

"I don't know. We'll just have to pray about . . ."

"Pray about it!" Sarah snorted. "Oh, sure." She gulped, wishing her words back. Trust. Had to keep thinking about trust.

"Well, you certainly haven't gotten anywhere on your own. What harm could it do?"

Sarah changed the subject. "I called and put an ad in the newspaper. They said they'll mail us the bill."

Everyday Sarah met the mailman at the box, but no one responded to her ad. She called the shelters whenever she went to town, and asked everyone she talked with to keep an eye out for Cimmaron. Each day that passed lessened the chances that Cimmaron was still alive. Sarah grew more quiet.

The following Friday when Sarah leafed through the mail, she found a letter addressed to her. With a cry she ripped it open.

"We have a sorrel gelding at our place that may fit the description of your animal. Call . . ."

Sarah flew down the drive. She could check right away. It *had* to be Cimmaron. Then she remembered. The pickup was missing. Her mom had gone back to work. They wouldn't be able to go until tonight. And her father couldn't drive yet, even if they could take the Pinto to town.

With a groan, Sarah slumped on the steps.

"What's in the mail?" Dad called from the living room.

Sighing, Sarah got to her feet. *If only*—she thought as she took the mail in to her father. Mutely, she handed him the letter.

"Why so sad? That's good news."

"Yeah, but I want to go *now.*"

Dad rubbed his chin. "Sorry, but evening will come fast. Wait a minute—why don't you call Sam on the CB? See if he's going to town."

"Sam," Sarah stuttered in her excitement when Sam answered the call. "Are . . . are you going to town soon?"

"Wa-l-l, I can," Sam drawled. "Whatta ya need?"

"There's a place that might have Cimmaron. Oh, please, Sam. Mom won't be home until after six and I want . . ."

"Hang on," Sam said with a chuckle. "We'll go."

"Right now?"

"Yep, right now. I'll be over quick as I can git there."

Sam's old tan truck seemed to take forever, chugging into Toledo.

"I'll call from here," Sarah said when she and Sam reached a phone booth, "to get the address. They just gave a phone number."

Sarah's fingers shook as she dialed. Her heart sank as the phone rang—and rang—and rang. She hadn't even thought of the people not being home. As she started to hang up, she heard a faint "Hello?"

"Oh!" Sarah breathed into the receiver, "I didn't think anyone was there. I'm Sarah Sorenson. You answered the ad about my horse?"

Seconds later Sarah leaped into the truck, the paper with the address on it fluttering in her hand. "It's not too far from here. Look." She handed the paper to Sam.

"Yep," Sam nodded. "Easy, girl, your bouncing isn't gonna make this old heap go any faster."

Sarah laughed with him. *Cimmaron, Cimmaron,* her heart sang.

A barking collie met the truck at the gate. "It's OK," a jeans-clad woman signaled from the steps of the old farmhouse. "He's all bark."

Shivers of excitement chased each other up Sarah's back as Sam parked the truck.

"Right this way," the woman said. "I hope this is your horse. He's such a friendly animal." She pushed open the barn door. "We've been keeping him in here. He's been through a lot."

"Oh, please be Cimmaron," Sarah whispered as the three approached the stall.

"Hey, fella, you've got company," the woman called. A sorrel horse turned from pulling hay out of the manger. Sarah felt as though someone had hit her in the stomach. Instead of a white blaze from forehead to whiskery lips, the animal had a white star between his eyes.

"That's not Cimmaron," Sarah choked out. She dashed the tears from her eyes.

"Oh, I'm so sorry," the woman said. "I was sure hoping."

"So was I."

"Well, if I hear of another horse, I'll let you know."

"Uh, thanks anyway." Sarah dragged her body back to the truck. She leaned her head against the window, unable to respond to Sam's sympathetic pat on her arm.

This is it, she told herself. *Guess I just have to give up. But . . .*

That night at family devotions, Dad watched her, his eyes warm with compassion. She hadn't said a word since returning with Sam.

"Sarah," Dad said finally. "I think you have two choices, Either give up and admit Cimmaron is dead, or—" Sarah looked up at him. "Or—pray about it. I know you feel God has let you down. You're trying to convince yourself He doesn't even exist. But He promises that we can try Him. Ask Him to reveal Himself to us."

Sarah refused to look at her father again. Right now she didn't feel like hearing a sermon.

"Your mom said it best: 'What have you got to lose?' "

The silence stretched on—and on. Even the two little girls sat still for a change.

Slowly Sarah looked up at her father. His face glowed with love and caring. He was right. What did she have to lose? Her family had prayed for Jani and she was getting better. Sarah nodded.

"OK," she whispered. "Let's pray for Cimmaron."

With hands joined, each member of the family prayed for Cimmaron's safety. Sarah kept track of each person's prayers. She concentrated on their words, seeing Cimmaron in her mind.

"God," Sarah said haltingly when her turn came. "If You are real, I need to know that. I can't stand this confusion anymore. I—I guess I want to believe in You, but—" She paused. Pictures of Sunshine's calf flashed through her mind. "It's been so hard." Tears filled her eyes and brimmed over. She sniffed. "And—oh, please, please—I want Cimmaron back—so bad—please."

"Father, we thank You that we can call You Father," Dad continued after a long pause. "We claim Your promises about prayer. That You'll hear us and answer. We thank You and praise You now for Your answers for Sarah. Amen."

Sarah crawled into bed that night with her father's words whispering in her ear. *God does care*, something assured her as she slipped into sleep.

Two long days later, Mom opened the back door as she returned from work. "Sarah, come here a minute."

The sparkle in Mom's eye promised good news as Sarah put her book down and joined her mother in the kitchen.

"Today at the feed store, I saw this card posted." Mom pulled a three-by-five card from her purse.

> We have animals at our base north of Toledo. Angus, Hereford, and crossbred cattle; two bay, one black and two sorrel horses; three ponies; sheep, dogs, cats, and rabbits. Please claim them. Call . . . Signed the Washington State National Guard

"I called and . . ."

"And?"

"One of their geldings has two white socks and a blaze."

"Oh, Mother!" Sarah was afraid to believe her ears.

"Let's all go." Dad stumped in from the living room on his crutches. "Call the girls."

Kathy and Kim chattered as the truck drew near Toledo, then headed north. Sarah remembered the empty feeling when she saw the other horse. *No, don't think of that*, she ordered herself. *This time may be different.*

Army green and tan camouflaged trucks lined the driveway as the Sorensons pulled into the parking area. Helicopters rested in the field like huge, lazy bugs. Men in green fatigues worked on the trucks and choppers. A couple of men rested against one of the buildings. As the truck stopped, one of the fellows left his buddies and approached the pickup.

"What can I do for you folks?" the man asked with a pleasant smile.

"We called about a sorrel gelding?"

"Sure 'nuff, the animals are down this way, behind that building."

"Sarah, you go ahead. I'll wait with your dad," Mom suggested. "You girls may go too."

Halfway to the makeshift corral, Sarah whistled. Her two-tone, high-low call cut through the air. An answering whinny catapulted her into a run. She whistled again as she rounded the building. Cimmaron, his bones poking at his rough, patchy coat, trotted across the grass. He tossed his head, then nickered again.

Cimmaron nuzzled Sarah's shoulder as she crawled through the fence.

"You crazy animal." Sarah laughed, cried, and hugged him all at once. "Oh, you silly old horse. I've missed you so."

Kathy and Kim ran back to the truck, screaming, "It's *him*! It's Cimmaron!"

"Somebody must have been watching out for that horse," the officer said.

"I prayed for him," Sarah answered quietly.

"Well, God sure answered your prayer. Your horse was nearly dead when we pulled him from the mud down near the Cowlitz River."

"Clear down there?"

"They almost destroyed him, he was so far gone. But one of the men here is a real horse lover. He wanted to try saving him so . . ."

"Oh, I'm so glad," Sarah breathed.

"Then the vet pumped him full of antibiotics 'cause the poor beast had pneumonia. He's had a rough time, he has."

Sarah buried her face in Cimmaron's matted mane. "Oh, Cimmaron," she whispered. "It looks like God does care. He kept you alive and brought you back to me." The word *trust* floated through her mind. As she was learning to trust God, perhaps He would show her ways to help her parents trust her again. Maybe she could pray for that too. After all, He had answered their prayers for Cimmaron. If there was any way, she never wanted to see that awful look in her dad's eyes again. "Thank you, mister. We'll be back as soon as we can with a trailer. And thank the others for helping take care of him."

"I will." He patted Cimmaron's neck. "Makes it all worthwhile when we can have a happy ending like this."

"Trust me, Cim, I'll be right back." Sarah patted her horse one more time. "We'll be back soon." She trotted back to the truck. "Thank you, God."